LOU LOU & PEA

AND THE MURAL MYSTERY

LOU LOU & PEA

AND THE MURAL MYSTERY

Written by
JILL DIAMOND

Illustrated by
LESLEY VAMOS

FARRAR STRAUS GIROUX
New York

Farrar Straus Giroux Books for Young Readers
175 Fifth Avenue, New York 10010

Text copyright © 2016 by Jill Diamond
Illustrations copyright © 2016 by Lesley Frances Vamos
All rights reserved.
Printed in the United States of America
by LSC Communications US, LLC (Lakeside Classic), Harrisonburg, Virginia
Designed by Kristie Radwilowicz
First edition, 2016
10 9 8 7 6 5 4 3 2 1

mackids.com

Library of Congress Cataloging-in-Publication Data

Names: Diamond, Jill, 1978– author. | Vamos, Lesley, illustrator.
Title: Lou Lou and Pea and the mural mystery / Jill Diamond ; illustrated by
    Lesley Vamos.
Description: First edition. | New York : Farrar, Straus, Giroux, 2016. |
    Summary: "Two best friends with a flair for adventure use their
    gardening and art skills to catch a criminal during Día de los
    Muertos"—Provided by publisher.
Identifiers: LCCN 2015036151 | ISBN 9780374302955 (hardback) |
    ISBN 9780374302962 (ebook)
Subjects: | CYAC: Best friends—Fiction. | Friendship—Fiction. |
    All Souls' Day—Fiction. | Mexican Americans—Fiction. | Mystery and
    detective stories. | BISAC: JUVENILE FICTION / Social Issues / Friendship. |
    JUVENILE FICTION / People & Places / United States / Hispanic & Latino. |
    JUVENILE FICTION / Humorous Stories.
Classification: LCC PZ7.1.D498 Lo 2016 | DDC [Fic]—dc23
LC record available at https://lccn.loc.gov/2015036151

Our books may be purchased for promotional, educational, or business
use. Please contact your local bookseller or the Macmillan Corporate and
Premium Sales Department at (800) 221-7945 ext. 5442 or by e-mail at
MacmillanSpecialMarkets@macmillan.com.

Special thanks to Patricia Williams Sánchez
for her careful proofreading of the Spanish text

LOU LOU & PEA

AND THE MURAL MYSTERY

CHAPTER ONE
PSPP

It was 3:37 p.m. on Friday, and Lou Lou Bombay was where she belonged—in her sunlit garden, talking to her fall-blooming camellia.

"I love Fridays, Pinky," Lou Lou said as she pruned a stray branch. "It's not the weekend but it's the almost-weekend. When you know there are two empty days ahead and anything can happen." Lou Lou stood on her tiptoes to examine a cluster of magenta flowers in full bloom. Pinky was a marvelous specimen—a camellia of the autumn queen variety and taller than Lou Lou by a full two feet. Lou Lou reached high to check the glossy leaves for aphids and other insect pests. Finding none, she smiled and thought about the upcoming garden show.

"You're going to win Best in Show for Flowering Bushes and Shrubs this year, Pinky. I just know it!" said Lou Lou. "Hello Horticulture! Society Annual Conference, here we come!" A breeze blew through the garden, and one of Pinky's branches bobbed at Lou Lou in agreement.

Just then, Lou Lou heard a knock at the backyard gate.

"Gotta go, Pinky. Happy PSPP!" Pinky's branch bobbed again as if to say, *Happy PSPP to you, too.*

PSPP (Post-School-Pre-Parents) was a glorious hour and twenty-three minutes of Lou Lou's Friday. School was over for the week, and from the time Lou Lou hopped off the bus on Lucky Alley until her parents came home from work at their architecture office, she had the house and the afternoon almost entirely to herself. The only other person she was guaranteed to see was a small brown-haired girl wearing a crisp school uniform. She was standing outside the gate now.

"Hi, Pea! I mean, welcome to my humble garden, Miss Peacock Pearl." Lou Lou remembered to greet her best friend with customary PSPP formality.

"Thank you, Miss Lou Lou Bombay! I am very pleased to be here," Pea said.

"I do hope your journey was not long," said Lou Lou, although she knew it was only a ten-minute bus ride from Pea's school to Lou Lou's house.

"Not at all," Pea replied with a dismissive wave. "Shall we?"

"Yeah, I'm starving!" answered Lou Lou, forgetting her manners as usual. Pea blinked her bright blue eyes at her best friend. Unlike Lou Lou, Pea was always polite, although she was extra, *extra* polite during PSPP.

"I mean, certainly, my dear. Please come in for a bite to eat and a spot of tea." Lou Lou pointed at the little table at the edge of her backyard. She'd laid out tea and scones, a PSPP tradition born after a rainy day spent watching an old movie about dignified British ladies. Lou Lou and Pea had agreed that it would be quite lovely to have their own weekly afternoon tea and scones.

Pea sat down and wiped her hands on a navy handkerchief embroidered with her initials. Lou Lou poured tea into mismatched cups, added a sprig of fresh mint from her garden to each, and handed Pea the blue one.

"What interesting things happened at your school today, Miss Pearl?" Lou Lou asked. Lou Lou and Pea had once gone to the same neighborhood school where they met in the first week of first grade. But two years ago, right before third grade, Pea had transferred to a creative arts school to pursue her passions, painting and fashion design.

"We have a new teacher in my Fun with Textiles class and she called me 'Pea.'" She carefully spread jam on her scone, avoiding potential finger stickiness. Lou Lou, who was licking jam off her wrist, stared at Pea with wide eyes. "It was annoying!" added Pea, who seemed to be finished with formal speech for today.

"Mmyeah," Lou Lou sympathized, her mouth filled with scone. Only Pea's family and Lou Lou were allowed to use Pea's nickname. Lou Lou, on the other hand, preferred her nickname and insisted that no one was to call her Louise.

"But I got my new color swatch book!" Pea pulled *The Definitive Book of Color* from her schoolbag. Lou Lou leaned closer as Pea showed her the different shades.

"Lots of the purples have flower names!" Lou Lou observed as they looked at a swatch of violet and another of wisteria.

"I know," Pea said. "And there are so many beautiful blues. Cerulean, ultramarine, azure . . ."

The breeze picked up again and riffled the pages of the latest issue of the Hello Horticulture! Society magazine. Since Pea was still perusing the blue color swatches, Lou Lou couldn't resist a quick peek at the Perfect Perennials section of the magazine.

"And how was *your* day?" Pea asked.

Lou Lou looked up from an article about the underappreciated ornamental onion. Nothing that had happened to her at school seemed as interesting as the onion's resistance to deer, voles, and rabbits.

"Same old, same old. Kyle Longfellow was irritating.

The mac and cheese was cold at lunch. Danielle Desserts called me 'Lou Lou Loser' in front of our whole Science class. But I got an A-minus on my math test and an A on my book report."

Pea sipped her tea. "Danielle is always so childish. But that is good news about your grades. Are you almost ready for the Hello Horticulture! Society Annual Conference? It's only a few weeks away!"

"Yes! I'm going to photograph Pinky's flowers soon," Lou Lou said. "I went to see Juan at Green Thumb Nursery earlier this week. He has a customer with a forsythia who thinks he'll win the competition, but Juan says the forsythia doesn't have a chance with Pinky in the running!" She winked at her camellia.

"Wonderful, Lou Lou!" replied Pea. Gardening was too dirty for her taste but she supported her best friend. "Now how about a stroll?" Pea suggested another PSPP tradition.

"Certainly." Lou Lou drained the final drop from her cup.

"Candles or cupcakes?" Pea asked. Here was the usual dilemma.

Should they head to Cupcake Cabana for their favorite frosted treats, or should they pay Elmira the Candle Lady a visit?

Before Lou Lou could answer, Pea's phone rang.

"¡Hola, Mamá!" Pea said, answering the call. Then she frowned. "¿Qué? ¿Qué? ¿Magdalena? ¿Su vestido? ¡Pobrecita! Sí, Mamá. Hasta luego."

"What happened? Is Magdalena okay?" Lou Lou didn't speak a lot of Spanish, but she recognized Pea's cousin's name.

"Magdalena is fine, but her quinceañera dress is not," Pea replied. "It was in my tía Marie's car. She left the window open by mistake and when she came back from running errands, there was a giant purple stain down the front of the dress!"

"From what? A sudden purple rainstorm? A mad magician's purple spell?"

"Nothing that weird. My mother said it smelled like grape juice. On second thought, that *is* weird. Why would someone pour grape juice on a quinceañera dress through a car window?"

"I don't know," Lou Lou said. "Maybe it was an accident? Otherwise, it's a really mean thing to do."

"Hopefully, the dress is not ruined," said Pea.

"Magdalena's quinceañera is on Sunday! Tía Marie took the dress to Sparkle 'N Clean this morning, and now my mother wants me to pick it up before they close."

"I guess that means candles today," said Lou Lou. Sparkle 'N Clean was on the same block as the candle shop. "We'll get Magdalena's dress, then we'll visit Elmira. Don't worry, Pea. It will all work out!"

With that, it was decided. Before they left for their stroll, Lou Lou left a message for her mom and dad with the details of their afternoon plan. Then she took one last peek at Pinky.

"See you tomorrow morning," she said to her camellia. "Stay beautiful!"

I will, Lou Lou, a bobbing branch seemed to say in reply.

CHAPTER TWO
Sparkle 'N Not-So-Clean

Lou Lou and Pea walked the short distance to Sparkle 'N Clean along cracked sidewalks, stopping occasionally to pet neighbors' pugs and poodles. Although they lived in a city, their little neighborhood was close-knit like a small town. It was called El Corazón, because it was in the heart of the city and alive with culture and art. Lou Lou and Pea adored their community for the rainbow of buildings, some of which had the popular El Corazón murals painted on them. The people of El Corazón were friendly, and neighbors were always greeting Lou Lou and Pea on the street or from their front porches with a *Hello!* or a *¡Buenos días!* And El Corazón was well-known for its community celebrations that were filled with beauty and energy.

On the way to Sparkle 'N Clean, Lou Lou and Pea admired things they loved about their neighborhood, from Mrs. Thompson's wooden lawn flamingos to the shiny red-and-black vintage cars that were meticulously maintained by Mr. Martinez. El Corazón dazzled the eye with its variety and color.

As they arrived at Sparkle 'N Clean, Pea pointed at the window display.

"Look at that silver boa!" Sparkle 'N Clean was a fashion boutique as well as a laundry. "And the jeweled headband is exquisite," Pea said as they went inside. "You should wear it when you claim Pinky's blue ribbon at the Hello Horticulture! Society Annual Conference."

"Lou Lou and Peacock! Darlings, so wonderful to see you!" Thomas, the owner of Sparkle 'N Clean, was arranging elaborate brooches on a table in the corner. "Are you two here for some satin opera gloves? Or perhaps a feathered fascinator for your Halloween costumes?"

Lou Lou noticed Pea gazing longingly at the opera gloves. Lou Lou made a mental note for Pea's next

birthday. "No, we're just picking up Magdalena's quinceañera dress," Lou Lou said.

"Oh riiight." Thomas sounded hesitant. "I'll go fetch it." He disappeared into a maze of clothing racks while Lou Lou and Pea looked at hats. Pea picked out a velvet hat with ribbons and flowers.

"That's like something Ella Divine would wear," said Lou Lou.

"I know, so glamorous," Pea replied. The hat was perched precariously on her head. "We're still going to her show next Friday, right?" The singer was Pea's idol, and Lou Lou was Ella Divine's second biggest fan.

"Yes! My mom and dad—" Lou Lou was interrupted by Thomas sweeping out from behind a rack of jackets. He was carrying Magdalena's quinceañera dress with its layered tulle skirt and beaded bodice that was fit for a fairy-tale ball.

"I'm afraid there was nothing I could do." Thomas held up the dress for Lou Lou and Pea. On the front was a wicked spread of purple, like a big bruise. Pea's mouth fell open, and the velvet hat slipped off her head and sailed to the floor.

"But it's just grape juice. Surely there must be a way . . ." Pea's voice grew quiet.

"Darling, I *wish* this was just grape juice. That would have been a snap, a breeze, nothing at all!" Thomas replied, waving his hand and wiggling his fingers. "But no no no. This was something much more vicious. One part grape juice, two parts DYE." Thomas said the last word in the voice of an old movie villain.

"Someone poured dye on Magdalena's dress?" Lou Lou could hardly believe it. "Who would do something so awful?"

"I haven't a clue," Thomas said. "But mark my words, whoever ruined this dress wanted it to stay ruined. What a shame! It was such a lovely shade of lemon yellow. Your prima has very good taste, Peacock."

Pea nodded. "Her quinceañera is in Limonero Park. She chose that color to match the lemon trees."

"What's Magdalena going to do?" Lou Lou looked at Pea.

"I don't know." Pea looked dismayed. "She will be really upset, that's for certain. There's not enough time for Tía Marie to make a new one." She reached for the huge dress, careful to avoid touching the stain. Because of its giant size, the dress hid Pea almost entirely—Lou Lou could barely see her two blue eyes peeking out over a cloud of yellow fabric.

"Please tell your tía that I'm sorry, Peacock. I spent half the morning soaking and scrubbing," Thomas said. "No charge."

"Thank you, Thomas," Pea replied.

"Of course, darling. If Magdalena needs a new dress, send her my way. I don't have anything lemon-colored, but I do have some gorgeous apricot taffeta that would look smashing on her."

Outside of Sparkle 'N Clean, Pea stared forlornly at the ruined bundle.

"C'mon," Lou Lou said, nodding in the direction of the candle shop. "Elmira is a genius at fixing problems! I bet she can help."

CHAPTER THREE
Elmira the Candle Lady
(Part One)

"Brrr!" Lou Lou buttoned up her coat as they walked down the block. The October day had been sunny and warm when they left Lucky Alley. But outside the candle shop, the wind picked up and Lou Lou's golden-brown curls whipped around her face.

The tiny candle shop was nestled between Manny's Bodega and Chilly Refrigerator Repair. The candle shop's official name was La Fortuna Candle Emporium, but everyone just called it the candle shop. An unremarkable building with faded paint, it was not much to look at from the outside. Still, the flames that danced in the window promised intrigue and warm memories. Lou Lou and Pea had spent many afternoons in the shop listening to Elmira's stories and advice. Lou Lou read aloud the shop's paper sign that she'd seen countless times: "SE VENDE LUZ Y SUERTE."

"We certainly need light and luck today to help Magdalena," Pea said.

A bell chimed overhead as Lou Lou and Pea entered the store. They were greeted by the aroma of smoldering incense and candles that smelled of jasmine, vanilla, and hot chilies. The candles, which were tall pillars flickering in glass holders, brightened the otherwise dark shop. They were every color of the rainbow and various shades in between, and they were decorated with writing and images. Lou Lou liked all the candle hues. But blue was Pea's signature color, as it matched her eyes and her name. She loved the candles that ranged from the light blue of a robin's egg to the dark blue of the early-night sky.

While they waited for Elmira to emerge from the back room, Lou Lou moved along one of the shelves, running her fingers over the smooth rims of the candleholders. Each candle made a different promise in pictures and Spanish words. Many of the words were still unfamiliar to Lou Lou, but she knew that the silver Buena Suerte candle, with its picture of a horseshoe, was for good luck. And the red Amor candle, with the heart, was for love. She paused at a yellow candle that showed a smiling face and read *Buena Salud*.

"Good salad? Why would anyone need a good salad candle?" Lou Lou held it up for Pea to see. Her best friend smiled.

"*Salud* means health, not salad."

"Oh, right," Lou Lou said. She hoped that someday she would speak Spanish as well as Pea. Pea was fluent because her mother, who was Mexican, spoke Spanish at home. Lou Lou wandered over to the green candle on the shop's counter. The dollar sign on the holder gave the meaning away—Riqueza, wealth.

"¡Hola, niñas!" Lou Lou and Pea heard Elmira's scratchy voice before they saw her face. The Candle Lady appeared through the curtain behind the counter.

Elmira had been selling candles for as long as Lou Lou could remember. Nearly everyone in the neighborhood relied on the Candle Lady to grant wishes and cure ailments, including Lou Lou and Pea. Elmira always lent a sympathetic ear to her customers and

recommended appropriate candles. But Lou Lou and Pea visited Elmira even when they had no need for a candle. They loved the Candle Lady's mysterious ways and they valued her wisdom and advice. She was always interested in problems and ready to cheer on accomplishments.

"How are things with you two? ¿Están bien?" Elmira asked. She was short and squat, and appeared older than Lou Lou's parents but younger than her grandparents. She favored gauzy garments and robes that she draped over herself in creative ways. Today she wore swaths of maroon silk.

"Muy bien, Elmira. ¿Y usted?" Lou Lou replied. Pea nodded at Lou Lou's Spanish, and Lou Lou felt a twinge of pride.

"Bien, gracias," said the Candle Lady. "It is always lovely to see you both. But I gather you are here today for my help with un problema."

Elmira seemed to know when people were just browsing for something they *might* need. In those cases, she would chat for a bit and then recommend a basic purple Felicidad candle to bring happiness. But Elmira could also tell when customers wanted something specific— the right candle to cure a cold or get a good grade in math. Elmira was so talented, she often made appropriate suggestions before customers began their tales of hope or woe. Sometimes she even helped people with problems they didn't know they had. Lou Lou, hoping to learn a few psychic tricks, had asked Elmira how she came to have her mystic knowledge. Elmira had simply answered, "Tengo la intuición." I have the intuition.

Now Elmira pointed to the dress in Pea's arms. "For a quinceañera, Peacock Pearl? Not yours, I presume. Cinco años más before you're fifteen. But it looks like you're left dealing with a destroyed-dress disaster!"

"It's her prima Magdalena's dress," Lou Lou replied. "Can you help, Elmira? Thomas at Sparkle 'N Clean says it's ruined and the quinceañera is on Sunday!"

"I am so sorry for Magdalena!" Elmira said. "Sí, you did the right thing by coming to me. I recommend a

Belleza candle to ensure that she finds a suitable new dress and looks beautiful on her big day." Elmira pulled from the shelf a pink candle with a picture of a woman holding a mirror.

"I'll take it. Gracias, Elmira," Pea said, then handed Lou Lou the dress so she could find money in her pocket.

Lou Lou admired her best friend's generosity as Pea shelled out half her allowance for her cousin's candle.

"Next time, send your prima here before troubles befall her so I can make certain she is protected. After all, prevention is the best remedy for misfortune."

"Voy a recordar que." Pea agreed to remember Elmira's suggestion. "Maybe you should get a candle for your garden," she said to Lou Lou. "I know you've had a bountiful year, but just to make sure that you win the Hello Horticulture! Society top honor."

"That's right!" Elmira clapped her hands and her eyes shone. "You are slated to win a camellia competition, Lou Lou Bombay. What fantastic flower fortune! Perhaps consider this one." Elmira pointed to a green candle. Its glass holder had a flower on it and the word *Crecer*. "It will help you avoid horrible horticulture hurdles."

"It means 'to grow,'" Pea translated.

"A candle for my garden is a good idea, Pea, but Pinky is already a blue-ribbon shoo-in," Lou Lou said. "Thanks anyway, Elmira. It's nice of you to recommend something." Lou Lou remembered to be polite, like Pea was always telling her.

"Of course," replied the Candle Lady, reaching across the counter to squeeze Lou Lou's hand. "Hasta luego, niñas, and please give my best wishes to Magdalena!"

"¡Adiós!" Lou Lou and Pea replied as they closed the shop door behind them.

"We had better head home so I can explain this to my mother." Pea took the stained dress back from Lou Lou.

"It's too bad Thomas couldn't get the stain out," Lou Lou said. "But Elmira was able to help with a candle, so at least the afternoon has a bright side!"

As they walked out into the waning sun, Lou Lou thought about the other bright side to the afternoon— Pinky's beauty. Elmira was right, Lou Lou did have fantastic flower fortune. Once I win that ribbon, she thought, the horticulture world will know the name Lou Lou Bombay!

CHAPTER FOUR
Helado the Bunny

Lou Lou and Pea took a different route home to see some of the finest art in the world—El Corazón's dazzling community-created murals. The murals bloomed throughout the neighborhood like the flowers in Lou Lou's garden, and they were painted by different artists in all styles. Pea had even worked on one as a class project. There were at least a hundred different murals in El Corazón. Lou Lou and Pea had tried to count them once but lost track. Lou Lou was sure that she and Pea were the murals' biggest admirers although the entire community was proud of the richly detailed art, which was well-known throughout the city. The murals covered fences, walls, and garage doors on many of the blocks. They showed elaborate scenes that included tigers, farmers, festivals, and village markets. Some depicted everyday life, while others showed visions from the artists' wildest imaginations. Each mural was brightly colored like the candles in Elmira's shop. There were rose reds, lemon yellows, emerald greens, midnight blacks, plum purples and, of course, peacock blues.

Lou Lou and Pea had been enjoying the colors and images of the nearby murals when they walked past Mrs. Krackle's house, which was surrounded by overgrown wild bushes. The bushes were a horticulture tragedy that seemed to be crying, *Help me, Lou Lou Bombay!*

"Proper pruning is not just for an award-winning appearance. It actually yields thicker foliage and more flowers," Lou Lou said, eyeing the crazy-looking azalea. She knew better than to attempt any uninvited work with her pruning shears because she was sure to be shooed away by angry Mrs. Krackle.

"The same is true for painting," Pea said. "Cleaning your brushes thoroughly makes them look presentable, but also helps you achieve a crisper finished project. Painted pears could look like funny-shaped apples if you don't wash all the red out of your bristles!" Then Pea changed the subject. "What should we do tomorrow?"

"Cupcake Cabana for sure!" Lou Lou replied.

"And we definitely need to start our Día de los Muertos preparations," Pea added.

Lou Lou and Pea never missed a special occasion. Birthdays were celebrated with fancy dresses and pineapple pizza. On Valentine's Day, they made gigantic paper hearts and taped them to the front doors of friends and neighbors. Last year, they'd even remembered Flag Day and decided to sew their own flag—a combination of American, Mexican, and pirate—for Lou Lou's home. Just as Lou Lou had climbed halfway out an upper window to hang the flag, her mom had spotted her. The flag now flew from the back porch instead.

While they made sure that no occasion went unobserved, for Lou Lou and Pea, the Mexican Day of the Dead celebration was particularly special. Día de los Muertos lasted three days, from October 31, the same day as Halloween, through November 2. On the final day, El Corazón filled with kids and adults remembering friends, family, and even pets that had passed away to the spirit world. But instead of being a sorrowful occasion, it was a celebration full of colors and candles, memories and marigolds.

The crowning event of Día de los Muertos was the procession. At twilight, the streets around Lucky Alley would be packed with people and their elaborate altars displaying candles, mementos, favorite foods, and photos of departed loved ones. Flowers were abundant, particularly marigolds, which were used to guide spirits to their altars. Many people even painted their faces to look like skeletons for the procession. Lou Lou and Pea had spent a long time perfecting their bony look by practicing with one of Lou Lou's mom's worn-down eyeliners and some white face makeup. The finishing touch was elaborate outfits, the more colorful the better. Pea's fashion expertise and sewing skills guaranteed that she and Lou Lou always created something amazing to wear.

"I have some great ideas for the procession this year—" Pea began, but Lou Lou grabbed her arm.

"Wait, we almost forgot to say hello to one of our favorites." Lou Lou stopped in front of a vibrant mural of a woman riding a horse in a field of tall grass and flowers. The woman's hair encircled her head in a windy halo of brushstrokes, and the horse's mane blew wildly

off his neck. Lou Lou and Pea had named many of the murals and they called this one *Lady Carmen Rides Bonito*.

"Hello, Lady Carmen," Lou Lou said to the beautiful rider.

"Hola, señorita," Pea said.

With their greetings spoken, they were ready to move on. Then something in the mural caught Lou Lou's eye. In the midst of a bloom of windblown daisies was a snow-white bunny with orange-yellow eyes that stared out sadly from the painting. Lou Lou had gazed upon this mural countless times and never noticed a bunny.

"Do you remember that?" she asked Pea, pointing at the furry creature.

Pea squinted. "No. And I know this mural so well, I could redraw it in my sleep. Though I guess we could have overlooked it since it's so small," Pea replied.

"No way. I think someone must have added it recently," Lou Lou said. "That's strange."

"The murals do change sometimes," Pea reminded Lou Lou. "Like when they turned that old building on Twentieth Street into the Estrella Theater and painted an opera scene over the fish mural."

"True," replied Lou Lou. "But usually the whole picture changes, not just one detail. The bunny's eyes are such an odd color, aren't they?" she observed.

"Yes, it's amber," said Pea, showing Lou Lou a matching color swatch in her new book.

"Amber," Lou Lou repeated, staring at the bunny's mournful expression.

"The bunny needs a name. How about Blanco?" Pea suggested.

"Naw, too obvious." Even Lou Lou knew that *blanco* means white in Spanish. "What about Helado since that means ice?"

"That is the word for ice cream. I like it, though." Pea giggled. "Helado it is."

Just in time for the end of PSPP, Lou Lou and Pea turned a corner and Lou Lou's house, the SS *Lucky Alley*, came into view. Lou Lou's home reflected her dad's passion for ships at sea, which Peter Bombay had inherited from a long line of Bombay sailors. The exterior was boat shaped and painted a shiny red with white trim around the porthole windows. Above the front door was a carved wooden mermaid figurehead that Lou Lou had named Serena.

Stepping inside the SS *Lucky Alley* meant entering a

world of ocean and sky. The walls were the many colors of the sea. Ceilings looked like the sky—the kitchen was stormy, the living room was sunny with cotton-ball clouds, and constellations of stars shone down into the bedrooms. Over the mantel hung photos of blurry dark shapes taken by Lou Lou's dad on a whale-watching trip. A rope ladder in the hallway led to a small room at the tiptop of the house. It had slanted ceilings and a porthole window through which pirates or the mail lady might be spotted. This was the ship's crow's nest, and more important, it was also Lou Lou's bedroom. All in all, the SS *Lucky Alley* was as close to a firsthand seafaring experience as a landlubber could get.

"Ahoy," Lou Lou whispered to her home when they entered. Although she wasn't as ocean-obsessed as her dad, Lou Lou loved the SS *Lucky Alley*.

It was almost time for Pea to go home, so they went into the living room to wait. Light poured through the windows as Lou Lou flung open the heavy canvas curtains crafted from old sails. The foghorn doorbell sounded.

"That's probably my mother," said Pea, gathering up Magdalena's dress and the Belleza candle.

Sylvia Pearl was waiting patiently on the front steps

to take Pea to their home on the far side of the neighborhood. She took one look at the dress and put her
hand over her eyes.

"The stain didn't come out? ¡Qué horror!"

"Sorry, Mamá."

But when Pea's mother saw the candle, she smiled. "It was nice of you to think of your prima, mija. Ándale. Time to go."

Lou Lou and Pea said their *See you tomorrow*s, and Lou Lou's parents arrived at the SS *Lucky Alley* a few minutes later. Lou Lou spent the evening diagramming her plans for fall plantings in her garden and daydreaming about pinning a Hello Horticulture! Society Flowering Bushes and Shrubs blue ribbon on a stake next to Pinky.

CHAPTER FIVE
Saturday in the Garden

That Saturday started like countless others. By seventhirty, Lou Lou was awake, dressed, and down the crow's nest ladder. She turned the big wooden ship's wheel that opened her fridge and gulped orange juice from the carton. Her dad's voice, commanding *Use a glass,* echoed in her head. But he was still asleep, and besides, she'd seen enough movies about sailors to know that they didn't all have perfect manners.

Then came the best part of Lou Lou's Saturday— visiting her plants and flowers in the soft morning sun. Although not everything was growing this season, she still made sure to greet each section of her garden using the names she'd given them.

"Good morning, Bouquet Blooms!" Lou Lou said as she skipped alongside the earthy bed of bulbs that bore colorful spring flowers—daffodils, tulips, and hyacinths.

"Hello, Summer Weirds!" Lou Lou remembered the unusual blooms from last season—goblin blanket flower, coreopsis moonbeam, and pink jewel fleabane.

"Greetings, Eats and Cures!" She couldn't overlook the variety of herbs and remedies, including mint for PSPP tea, basil for spaghetti sauce, soothing chamomile, and echinacea to ease colds.

"It's your time to shine, Fancy Fall Florals!" Lou Lou said to the current season's array of asters, toad lilies, and perennial sunflowers.

Although she loved every plant and flower in her garden, she cherished spending Saturdays with Pinky in particular. Today, Lou Lou was excited to check the progress of Pinky's flowers. At the height of their bloom, she would photograph Pinky for the competition. The photos had to be perfect. Lou Lou had wanted that blue ribbon since she was old enough to grow her first rhododendron.

Lou Lou made her way toward the camellia, which was hidden in the partial shade of the avocado tree. But before she reached Pinky, she heard the *bang, bang, bang* of one hard object striking another. The sound was coming from Mr. Gray's yard next door. Lou Lou turned back and peered over the wooden fence that lined her backyard, expecting to see her grumpy neighbor in his bathrobe that was the same color as his last name. Instead, she spied a boy reclining on an ancient lawn chair, reading a comic book. Lou Lou eyed him warily until he looked in her direction.

"Hiya," said the boy.

"Hiya, yourself," Lou Lou replied. She continued to stare with narrowed eyes. The boy grinned, unfazed. He had bright blue spiky hair and brown eyes, and was wearing black boots and a studded leather bracelet on his left wrist. Lou Lou guessed that he was her age or a little older.

"Jeremy, that's me," said the boy. His overly friendly tone didn't suit his look. "And you are . . . ?"

"Lou Lou . . . Lou Lou Bombay. Where's Mr. Gray? And what are you doing in his yard?"

"Mr. Gray?" Jeremy seemed confused. "Oh, right—the old guy. He went on a long vacation."

Lou Lou pictured Mr. Gray eating a pastry at a café in Paris, or on a boat cruising the Amazon looking for exotic birds. But the images didn't fit her neighbor, who rarely even left his house.

"Vacation?" she asked skeptically. "Mr. Gray?"

"Yeah, he's visiting his sister in Toledo . . . or something like that. Anyway, I just moved here and my parents are renting his house for a few weeks until we find one of our own. What are *you* doing here?"

"I live here." Lou Lou used her confident "duh" voice. "Why did you move?" she asked. "Will you be going to school?"

"My parents grew up in this neighborhood and we still have family here. And, yeah, of course I'm going to school. Gotta work on my smarts!" Jeremy tapped his head and grinned. Lou Lou didn't smile back. Something about this boy seemed weird, but she couldn't put her finger on exactly what. "Actually, I'm starting on Monday at El Corazón Public."

Lou Lou's ears prickled. That was her school!

"What grade?" she asked.

"Sixth," he said. Lou Lou relaxed a little. At least he wasn't in her class.

"Hey, what was all that noise?" Lou Lou remembered

the *bang*s that had gotten her attention in the first place.

"Oh, that," Jeremy said unhelpfully. He gestured at a hammer lying in the grass. "I was just working on the old guy's fence."

"I didn't know the fence was broken," replied Lou Lou.

"Yeah, it wasn't." Jeremy picked up the hammer and struck the metal leg of the lawn chair, grinning at the noise.

"Then why—oh, never mind. I have important stuff to do." She decided she'd had enough of this strange boy for one morning, but tried to have some manners. "Good to meet you, though, I guess."

"See ya soon!" Jeremy winked.

Lou Lou hurried to the avocado tree, as her visit with Pinky was overdue. But when she finally gazed upon her beloved autumn queen camellia, she gasped and reeled in horror.

"Oh, Pinky! How awful!" Lou Lou wailed. Just yesterday, Pinky had been the picture of magenta-and-green health. But now, most of the beautiful blooms had fallen off and were shriveling in the grass. The few flowers that remained were drooping and sad, as if they would drop any minute to join their fallen comrades. The camellia's branches, which had once wished Lou Lou a happy PSPP, were now on the ground in a splintered heap. And the formerly lush leaves were wrinkled and browning at the tips. What little remained of the plant bowed toward the lawn in despair.

"What happened to you, Pinky?" Lou Lou hated crying, but she couldn't stop the fat tears that rolled down her cheeks. She brushed them away and suppressed a sob so she could assess the possible causes of the Pinky tragedy. She'd just yesterday checked for insect pests and found none. The weather that week had been good for horticulture—enough

rain and not too hot or cold. Despite the avocado tree that towered next to it, the camellia still got enough sun. With these culprits eliminated, all that remained was the mischief of an animal or human. The neighborhood cats liked to hide beneath Pinky and sniff at its leaves but they never bothered the camellia. This only left the sinister handiwork of a *person.*

Lou Lou put her nose to the ground and sniffed.

"Bleach and vinegar!" she cried. These were deadly poisons for a camellia, and Lou Lou's hopes for Pinky's recovery sank. On closer inspection, Lou Lou saw that Pinky's broken branches had been knocked off. Someone had definitely been out to get her plant! There was no way Pinky was in the running for a Flowering Bushes and Shrubs blue ribbon now, unless there was an award for saddest camellia.

The sob finally escaped from deep in Lou Lou's throat.

"You've been assaulted, Pinky! Battered and poisoned," Lou Lou growled. "I swear on all that is green and growing that I will avenge this crime!"

It was then that Lou Lou remembered the hammer that Jeremy claimed he had used to fix the unbroken fence. A few good swings and he could have easily knocked off Pinky's branches. And bleach and vinegar could have come from Mr. Gray's kitchen. Lou Lou ran back to the fence and glared into her neighbor's yard, but all she saw were the rusty old lawn chairs.

Jeremy was nowhere to be seen.

CHAPTER SIX
Elmira the Candle Lady
(Part Two)

Lou Lou's mom, Jane Bombay, was still in a sleepy daze when Lou Lou stormed into the SS *Lucky Alley* kitchen. She moved into Lou Lou's path just in time for Lou Lou to crash into her, spilling Jane's coffee all over her fuzzy bathrobe.

"Jeepers, young lady! Try to be more careful—" Lou Lou's mom stopped in mid-scold, for it was clear that something was very wrong with her daughter. Lou Lou's hazel eyes were little slits and her hands were clenched at her sides. But most telling were her ears.

Whenever Lou Lou was excited or upset, they tingled and burned, turning pink, then red. The more worked up she got, the hotter and redder her ears became. Right now they were the color of strawberries.

Lou Lou paused. She said *chrysanthemum* three times in her head, a method she used to control her anger. "I'm sorry, Mom. It's just . . . something bad has happened, and I think Pinky is dying."

"Oh, Lou Lou! That's terrible! What can I do?" her mom asked. "I know I'm not very good at gardening, but I am always happy to be your horticulture sidekick." Lou Lou wished it were that simple. But this was a job for experts.

"I need to go to Green Thumb. Is that okay?" asked Lou Lou before she remembered that Juan didn't open the nursery until nine-thirty. But the candle shop was open earlier and if anyone besides Juan could help, it would be Elmira. "Actually, I need to go to the candle shop first and then to Green Thumb. Please."

"I was making banana pancakes," Lou Lou's mom replied. "But I guess they can wait." A bowl of fluffy flour mixture sat on the counter. Banana pancakes with walnuts swimming in a lake of maple syrup were a Jane Bombay Saturday specialty that Lou Lou hated to miss. But her mom was right—pancakes could wait and Pinky could not.

"I'll be quick, Mom! Pinky really needs help," Lou Lou said.

"I understand, honey. Do you want me to come? I don't like you wandering around by yourself."

"I won't be on my own for long," Lou Lou replied. "I'll call Pea and have her meet me."

"Okay. Make sure you're home in an hour and, here, take my phone." Lou Lou nodded and rushed out the door. On the way to the candle shop, she dialed Pea.

"Hello?" Pea's father, Henry Pearl, answered.

"Hi, it's Lou Lou. Is Pea up? It's really important!"

"She's not, but I was just about to wake her. She'll sleep all morning if I don't. Hold on a minute."

"Actually, can you just ask her to meet me at Elmira's as soon as possible? Thanks, Henry!" Lou Lou didn't wait for a reply.

When Lou Lou arrived at the candle shop, Elmira's door was locked. There were still ten minutes until the shop opened, so Lou Lou sat on the sidewalk and tapped her foot on the concrete, running through crime scenarios in her head. Had Jeremy assaulted Pinky with poisons and a hammer? It seemed possible, but he had no motive that she knew of. Maybe it was someone else, someone who wanted the blue ribbon. There was that man with the forsythia who always bragged to Juan. Or it could have been the girl who'd won last year with her hydrangea. But she'd seemed really nice and had given Lou Lou some helpful fertilizer tips.

Lou Lou was still thinking about culprits when Pea's father dropped her off. Pea looked uncharacteristically disheveled from the morning rush out the door. She'd missed buttons on her coat, her scarf was askew, and a section of her hair was matted.

"Lou Lou, what on earth is going on?" Pea asked, squatting down next to her while being careful not to touch the dirty pavement. She worked her hair into a neat braid, adjusted her scarf, and rebuttoned her coat.

"Oh, Pea. It's just awful. Horrific!" Lou Lou cried. Before she could explain, she heard the *click* of a lock behind her. The candle shop was open for business. Rushing inside, Lou Lou nearly tripped over the Candle Lady.

"Can you help me, Elmira? Who did this? And *why*? Why would someone hurt Pinky, my poor camellia? I'm never going to win a blue ribbon now!"

Pea raised her eyebrows, finally understanding why Lou Lou was so upset.

"¡Qué lástima, Lou Lou Bombay!" Elmira clucked

and shook her head. "I am sorry for your woes. I know how much you love esa camelia preciosa. And the competition is right around the corner!" The Candle Lady patted Lou Lou's arm. "Plant problems are painfully puzzling."

"Do you think a candle can help?" Lou Lou asked.

"I certainly hope so," replied Elmira. "Please, that one." The Candle Lady pointed at the Crecer candle that Lou Lou had declined yesterday. "Since you are a good friend and have suffered such a catastrophic camellia calamity, twenty percent off."

"Thank you, Elmira. Does your intuition tell you anything about who would harm Pinky?" she asked. "Was it one of my Hello Horticulture! Society competitors? Or maybe my new neighbor?" Lou Lou thought back to Jeremy's suspicious hammering.

"I wish I could help you, but no one is coming to mind. Unfortunately my deepest sympathies and the candle are all I can offer," Elmira said, her brow furrowed with concern.

Lou Lou sighed and took the green candle from the dusty shelf. Maybe it could magically revive Pinky. She pulled a fistful of crumpled dollars from her pocket and counted them out. For Lou Lou, money was measured in two-dollar cupcakes, and this candle had just set her back four vanilla buttercreams. But it was worth it if it would save her camellia.

Realizing that Lou Lou still owed Elmira more, Pea handed the Candle Lady two neatly folded bills.

"Pea—" Lou Lou started to protest.

"It's okay, I want to help. And I got my allowance today."

"Thanks, Pea. From me *and* Pinky."

"Sí, muchas gracias." Elmira put the money into the cash register. "And you, Peacock Pearl . . . I sense you may be facing another feisty feline fiasco."

This was correct. Pea's mean cats, Uno (the black cat) and Dos (the white cat), hated each other and were in a hissy war.

"Tiene razón, Elmira," Pea answered. "But I still

have the Amistad candle I bought a few months ago. The cats are not exactly friends now, but when I burn it, Uno hides under the couch and Dos curls up behind the bookshelf. It keeps them from fighting, so it seems to be working!"

"Muy bien," Elmira replied. Then she offered a bit of her mystical wisdom: "Shine a light on a problem and you'll have an answer." Before she disappeared behind the curtain, the Candle Lady said, "Again, I am very sorry about your plant. Buena suerte."

Lou Lou looked at the Crecer candle in her hands. Would its light be the answer to Pinky's recovery? She wasn't sure, but she was willing to try anything.

"Please bring Pinky back," she whispered.

CHAPTER SEVEN
A Planticide!

Lou Lou paced the length of the tiny crow's nest. It had been exactly four hours and thirty-one minutes since she started her Saturday with enthusiasm. But so much had changed in that time and Lou Lou had spent much of it fuming, puzzling, and running back and forth between her room and her garden to check for other signs of plant assault or mischief. Pea watched from the bed, coughing occasionally at the mixture of smoke and sweetgrass from the Crecer candle.

Lou Lou knew only a miracle could bring Pinky back to life. They'd stopped at Green Thumb after leaving the candle shop. Juan, although devastated to hear of the attack on Pinky, couldn't think of a solution. Still, Lou Lou kept her eyes on the window, hoping she'd see bright blooms reappear on her beloved camellia. But Pinky was in the same sorry state and a recovery seemed doubtful. Lou Lou's Flowering Bushes and Shrubs blue-ribbon dreams were dying alongside her plant. She threw up her hands and flopped down next to Pea, almost toppling a plate of half-eaten cucumber sandwiches.

"Lou Lou," Pea said soothingly. "I think you need to take your mind off things. Maybe we should go for a walk? I could treat you to Cupcake Cabana."

"Take my mind off things!" seethed Lou Lou. She put her cool hands over her scorching ears. "There has been an unthinkable camellia crime. This isn't merely a *thing*! It's a murder—a homicide. No, a *planticide!*"

"I understand, and I am trying to help." Pea spoke gently despite her friend's anger. She patted Lou Lou's arm and Lou Lou's breathing slowed.

Chrysanthemum, chrysanthemum, chrysanthemum, Lou Lou said to herself. "Sorry, Pea. I didn't mean to snap at you. I'm just so furious, I could scream."

"Even more reason to go out," said Pea. "You can have a nice long scream in Limonero Park. Plus, I hear that cupcakes can help with planticide investigations.

People think more clearly when their stomachs are full of frosting."

"I guess you're right," said Lou Lou. She'd skipped breakfast and barely touched her sandwich, so her mouth watered at the thought of Cupcake Cabana. Sometimes vanilla buttercream was the best immediate solution for a serious problem.

"Good, it's settled." Pea made for the rope ladder before Lou Lou could change her mind. Lou Lou looked out the window one last time to check on her garden. Finding nothing disturbed, she blew out the Crecer candle and followed in Pea's footsteps.

After they stopped at Cupcake Cabana, Lou Lou and Pea headed toward the park. Turning a corner, they nearly ran into a ruddy-faced boy.

"Whoa!" said Kyle Longfellow.

"Whoa yourself, Kyle," Pea replied as she smoothed her outfit. Kyle was in the same grade as Lou Lou and Pea, and they'd known him forever. Kyle always teased Pea. Pea insisted he was just being childish, but Lou Lou thought he might have a crush on her.

"Peacock Pearl is a stupid girl," Kyle said in a

singsong voice, staring at Pea to make sure he had her attention.

"Look at Kyle, he's so vile," said Lou Lou. Kyle seemed to notice Lou Lou for the first time. He stuck out his tongue in reply.

"Did you escape from the zoo today?" Kyle asked, eyeing Pea's royal-blue coat with its leopard-print pockets.

"What a clever joke, Kyle," Pea said sarcastically. "At least I don't look like a bumblebee." She pointed at Kyle's black-and-yellow striped sweater.

Kyle's face turned tomato red. "It's not a bumblebee sweater! These are Comet Cop's favorite colors, so I wear them when I'm on space patrol."

Lou Lou rolled her eyes. Kyle was always playing make-believe. He wanted to be an interplanetary police officer when he grew up, just like his favorite super-hero, Comet Cop.

Lou Lou changed the subject. "Kyle, you didn't happen to see anyone suspicious near my garden this morning, did you? I mean, when you were out on your space patrol?" Kyle was always spying on people, and if he had information about Pinky's attack, Lou Lou wanted to know.

"That's a negative, Lou Lou Bombay," Kyle said. "But

I'll keep a lookout. If I do see anyone suspicious, I can stop them with my cosmic kung fu or my meteor blaster."

"Yeah, whatever," Lou Lou said.

"Hey, you never know when you might need my protection." Kyle stole a glance at Pea. "Something could happen at any time . . . BOO!" Kyle jumped at Pea to scare her. She stood still.

"Let's go," Lou Lou said to Pea. She'd had enough of Kyle Longfellow for one day.

"Goodbye, Kyle," Pea said.

"Wait, you guys! Don't you want to hear about the arrests I made at school when I was on hall monitor duty?"

"Another time," Lou Lou said. The two friends waved to him as they hurried off.

It wasn't long before Lou Lou and Pea were in their favorite park, sitting cross-legged on their favorite bench with their favorite cupcakes. Being in Limonero Park made Lou Lou feel a bit better and she decided to save her angry scream for another time. Lou Lou had many fond memories of colorful El Corazón festivals and celebrations in the park. Like most of the neighborhood kids, she and Pea had been going there since they were little, and the sight of the shiny swing set and the lemon trees that ringed the park cooled Lou Lou's ears. The buttercream frosting helped, too.

"Tell me more about your new neighbor," Pea said. Lou Lou had mentioned Jeremy during her rant about potential suspects.

"He's kind of strange." Lou Lou told Pea about Jeremy's spiky blue hair, black boots, studded bracelet, and overly friendly personality.

"Maybe he is just genuinely nice," Pea suggested. "And his blue hair sounds pretty!"

"He seemed fake to me." Lou Lou revealed a mouthful of cupcake. "And it's suspicious that he moved here at the *very same time that Pinky was murdered*."

"Is that actually suspicious?" Pea asked. "People move to new places all the time."

"I think it's more than just a coincidence," Lou Lou said. "He also mentioned he has 'family' in the neighborhood." She made air quotes with her fingers. "But he didn't tell me who. Probably because there is no family—he made it up!"

Pea patted her napkin at stray frosting on her lip and pondered this.

"There's more. He had a hammer, Pea. A hammer! He said he was using it to work on Mr. Gray's fence, but the fence wasn't broken. What if he was killing poor Pinky right under my nose?" Lou Lou's voice grew quieter and her eyes began to fill with tears. Pea took Lou Lou's hand and gave it a sympathetic squeeze.

"True, it might have been him," Pea said. "But it could have been someone else, too. Either way we will figure out what happened." Lou Lou nodded and struggled not to cry. She glanced at Pea's blue watch.

"We better go. We told my mom we'd be home by three."

They gathered up their bags, cupcake wrappers, and kicked-off shoes that were scattered on the grass. As they were leaving, they heard footsteps fast approaching. It was Magdalena hurrying across the path through the park.

"Hey, chicas!" Magdalena called. Pea's cousin was tall with smooth chestnut hair cut into a bob and skin the color of honey.

"Hola, Prima," replied Pea. "¿Cómo estás? Did you get a new dress yet?" Magdalena almost always wore an expression that Lou Lou and Pea called her gold-medal smile since they were sure she'd win the Smile Olympics. But she frowned at the mention of her quinceañera dress.

"No, but I'm heading to Sparkle 'N Clean now."

"I'm really sorry about what happened," Lou Lou said.

"Thanks, Lou Lou. It's a total bummer. I was so excited to wear that dress tomorrow. It was such a beautiful color—a perfect match for a party here." Magdalena looked wistfully at the lemon trees. "It really hurts when something you love is destroyed."

Lou Lou knew exactly how that felt. "My camellia was killed today," she said.

"Pinky? Oh, Lou Lou, that is so sad!" Magdalena exclaimed. "Pea told me how excited you were about competing for the blue ribbon. It's weird that bad things happened to both of us this week."

"Do you have any idea who ruined your dress? Or why?" Lou Lou asked.

"I've been thinking about that," replied Magdalena. "I guess it could have been one of the mean girls in my grade."

Lou Lou could also relate to this. She thought of Danielle Desserts and her snooty-girl posse. Could they be behind Pinky's planticide?

"Or it could have just been some kid playing a cruel trick," Magdalena continued. "I've got a quart of revenge cranberry juice in my fridge for when I find out!"

"I hope the Belleza candle helps!" Pea said.

Magdalena's mouth finally turned up into her gold-medal smile. "I've been burning it ever since you gave it to me. Fingers and toes crossed," she said, walking off toward Sparkle 'N Clean.

CHAPTER EIGHT
School Is for the Birds

"I have an idea!" Pea said on the walk from Limonero Park to the SS *Lucky Alley*. "We should make an altar for Pinky. We'll carry it in the Día de los Muertos procession."

Lou Lou, who had been quiet and gloomy, perked up. "Great plan, Pea! If Pinky doesn't recover, of course."

"Oh, of course," Pea replied. "I didn't mean to . . ." She trailed off.

Lou Lou put an arm around Pea's shoulder. "It's okay. I've spent five whole years—half my life!—as a horticulture enthusiast. I know that Pinky's chances are slim. If we do make an altar, we'll have to do it soon. Día de los Muertos is coming right up!"

"We could redo Bisabuela Nellie's altar for Pinky," Pea suggested. "The frame already has flowers painted on it."

When Pea's great-grandmother Nelida Soto had passed away last year, Lou Lou helped Pea make a Día de los Muertos altar to remember her. They decorated the altar with painted flowers, crepe paper, a photo of Bisabuela Nellie in her favorite chair, and construction-paper dogs to symbolize Pea's great-grandmother's beloved terriers. Alongside Pea's family, Lou Lou and Pea had carried the altar in the twilight procession. Then they sat on Pea's front porch to eat pistachios, Bisabuela Nellie's favorite food, and tell each other her terrible jokes.

"But that altar is so special to you," replied Lou Lou.

"It is special. Even more reason to pass it along. We made it for someone *I* loved, now we can reuse it for something *you* loved. I want Pinky to have it, and I bet Bisabuela Nellie would, too."

"Thanks, Pea. That's really nice of you." Lou Lou hugged her best friend.

"We will just need to make a few changes." Pea had

her dreamy planning-an-art-project look on her face. "Maybe add more flowers, a photo, and some things that remind you of Pinky."

"My mom might even have perfume with camellia notes. We could spray the altar with it," Lou Lou suggested.

"What a wonderful idea. Bisabuela Nellie would be proud, Lou Lou," Pea said.

Lou Lou thought of one of Bisabuela Nellie's bad jokes. "Why shouldn't you write with a broken pencil?"

Pea grinned. "Because it's pointless! What kind of flower is on your face?" Pea asked.

"Tulips!" Lou Lou replied, and giggled, even though she'd heard the joke a hundred times. This was the first time Lou Lou had laughed since the morning's tragic events. A Día de los Muertos altar for Pinky was definitely a good idea.

Not far from Lou Lou's house, Lou Lou pointed to another favorite mural.

"We have to say hello to *School Is for the Birds*," she said. *School Is for the Birds* was a painting of a classroom filled with students looking at a map of the world. From the inside, the school looked like Lou Lou's, but the outside view revealed that it was in the middle of a jungle. Monkeys peered through tangled vines and an array of colorful birds perched on tree branches.

Lou Lou nodded to acknowledge the mural, then stopped short to examine it. Between two monkeys was a burst of lemon yellow and purple that had not been there before. But instead of being another bird amid the leaves, the new colors belonged to a familiar dress.

"Pea!" Lou Lou exclaimed. "It's a grape-juice-dyed quinceañera dress!"

"What?" Pea, who'd been brushing cupcake crumbs off the sleeve of her coat, looked at the painting with wide eyes. "Why is Magdalena's dress in the mural?"

"I dunno, but it's loco!" Lou Lou said. "You were right before that the murals change, but until now it's always been because someone replaces an entire old scene with a new one."

"It is also strange that someone painted a bad thing that *actually* happened," Pea added. "The murals are not usually so realistic."

"Something funny is definitely going on here, Pea. We need to figure out what it is! We're so good at sleuthing. Remember the treasure hunt in second grade when we found enough tamarindo candy to last us a year?"

Pea nodded. "We need to investigate," she agreed.

"The least we can do is find out what happened to my prima's beautiful dress!"

Pea is right, thought Lou Lou. They definitely needed to help Magdalena. Lou Lou also remembered Helado the bunny.

"I bet Helado is real, too, just like Magdalena's dress." As these words came from Lou Lou's mouth, she heard footsteps and rustling. A teenage girl emerged from a nearby alley. Her long hair was clipped back into a ponytail and she was wearing a skirt that was a waterfall of red-and-white ruffles. Lou Lou recognized her from an art show she'd attended with Pea.

"Pea, isn't that—"

"Rosa!" Pea finished. "I bet she designed that gorgeous skirt herself. She is so creative!"

"¡Hola, Rosa!" Pea said. Rosa looked in their direction.

"Hello, Peacock," Rosa called softly, and waved. "And hello . . ."

"I'm Lou Lou."

"Of course. La mejor amiga de Peacock." Rosa walked up to the girls. "Hola, Lou Lou."

"Your skirt is lovely. Did you make that?" Pea asked.

"Sí," replied Rosa.

"Maybe you can show me how you did the design?" Pea was always eager to polish her fashion skills.

"I'd be happy to, but right now I am late to meet a friend," Rosa said, her eyes darting off into the distance. "I have to go. Hasta luego." Rosa waved again and turned down the next alley.

"Rosa! Hold on a minute!" Lou Lou called, thinking maybe she'd seen who had changed the mural. But she was too late. Rosa was gone.

CHAPTER NINE
Suspect Sunday

On Sunday morning, Lou Lou went straight from her bed to check on her garden. The sight of her magnificent toad lilies, which seemed to have bloomed overnight, gave her hope. Maybe the Crecer candle had worked, and Pinky would come back from the dead with new buds. She closed her eyes and tried to will Pinky alive and well, envisioning a happy and healthy camellia.

Unfortunately, Lou Lou's hopes were crushed again when she peeked around the avocado tree. Pinky was even sadder and more withered than before. Looking back at the thriving toad lilies, Lou Lou felt a bit resentful.

After a thorough inspection, Lou Lou found no more signs of horticultural tampering. She trudged into the kitchen of the SS *Lucky Alley* and was greeted by a *whir, whir, whirring* noise and the aroma of cinnamon. These were the sounds and smells of pancakes in progress. Lou Lou's mom was at the stove, flipping circles of golden-brown batter.

"Banana pancakes on a Sunday?" Lou Lou was surprised. Her mom turned and smiled.

"You missed them yesterday so I thought we'd break tradition for once. Plus, I know you had a rough Saturday. How's Pinky?"

"Not good." Lou Lou's voice broke a little. "I don't think there's anything more I can do."

"I'm sorry." Her mom reached out and patted Lou Lou's curls. "It's unusual for one of your plants to die suddenly. I can't even keep grass alive, but you— you're a gardening genius. Have you figured out what happened?"

"Uh . . ." Lou Lou hesitated. Telling her mom she suspected a planticide certainly wasn't going to bring Pinky back. Instead, it could mess up Lou Lou and Pea's investigation by adding well-intentioned parents. She thought back to when she'd told her dad that Pea was afraid of sea lions and he'd put on a friendly-sea-lion costume to cure Pea of her fear. Poor Pea had hid in a closet for an hour. So Lou Lou wanted to handle the Pinky investigation *her* way. "I'm not entirely sure," Lou Lou replied. This was basically true since Lou Lou had yet to figure out the whole story.

"I can take you to Green Thumb this week and we can get you a new plant to replace—" Lou Lou's mom began.

"Nothing can replace Pinky, Mom!" Lou Lou immediately regretted her outburst. After all, her mom was just trying to be helpful.

"I understand," her mom replied. "If you feel ready for a new camellia, you just let me know. Now have some breakfast." She'd already set the table and left a little origami heart beside Lou Lou's plate. Jane had recently perfected her origami technique and could make just about anything from folded paper. She said it soothed her, like ocean sounds soothed Lou Lou's dad.

"Thanks, Mom." Lou Lou smiled.

When Lou Lou was eating her second helping of pancakes and working on her homework, her dad wandered into the kitchen.

"Good morning," he said, yawning and stretching in his blue-and-white striped pajamas dotted with little red sailboats.

"Hi, Dad." Lou Lou crunched on a walnut.

"Whatcha working on?"

"A story for English," replied Lou Lou. "We have to write scary tales for Halloween. Mine's about deadly nightshade. People thought witches used it to make flying ointment so they could fly to witch parties. Interesting, huh?" Lou Lou remembered something else. "Dad, can you drive me to the crafts store today?"

"Sure. I have to go out for groceries anyway," her dad answered. "Do you need Halloween decorations? We can turn this place into a ghost ship again!"

"No, I need some things for the procession," Lou Lou said. When she and Pea were little, Halloween had been a big deal, but now it was overshadowed by Día de los Muertos. Not that Lou Lou had anything *against* Halloween, she just felt as if she'd outgrown it, and preferred to celebrate Día de los Muertos. Especially this year, since she was mourning her beloved camellia.

Lou Lou's dad looked disappointed, and she remembered how much he loved decorating the SS *Lucky Alley*. "But we can pick up some Halloween decorations, too."

"Great!" Her dad clapped his hands. "I'll get dressed and we can leave."

Lou Lou finished her pancakes, ran her finger around

the plate, and licked off the last of the maple syrup. She realized that Magdalena's quinceañera was in a couple of hours so she picked up the phone and dialed Pea.

"Hello?" a familiar voice answered.

"Hi, Pea. It's me. Did Magdalena find a new dress?"

"Yes! It doesn't match the trees in Limonero Park but it is just as pretty as the first one."

"That's great! I guess the Belleza candle helped. Thank goodness for Elmira! Too bad the Crecer candle didn't work for Pinky."

"I know. I wish it had, Lou Lou. I can't talk for long. We are meeting my prima and my tía at Ruby's Beauty Parlor to get our hair styled before the party." Lou Lou heard the note of excitement in Pea's voice. Lou Lou admired elaborate hairstyles, but she couldn't imagine sitting still long enough to get one. "What are you going to do today?" Pea asked.

"My dad is taking me to the crafts store. I'll get some Día de los Muertos supplies. Anything you want?"

"I have plenty of scrap fabric and buttons. But I need some tassels. ¡Gracias!"

"¡Hasta banana!" Lou Lou replied, replacing the Spanish word for tomorrow, mañana. Pea laughed and Lou Lou hung up, just as her dad returned wearing his captain hat.

"Captain Peter, ready for our journey. Can we set sail now, First Mate Lou Lou?" Lou Lou rolled her eyes at her dad's goofiness, but then cracked a smile and followed him out to the car.

On their trip to the crafts store, Lou Lou and her dad passed by mural after colorful mural, including *Lady Carmen Rides Bonito*.

"Dad?" Lou Lou asked. "You know that mural with the woman on a horse on a windy day?"

"Is it on Nineteenth Street?" her dad asked.

"No."

"Is it next to Green Thumb?"

"No."

"Is it by your school?"

"No." Lou Lou was getting frustrated.

"Sorry, Lou Lou. I have no idea. There are so many murals I can't keep track." Lou Lou tried a different tactic.

"Well, have you noticed any of the murals changing in a weird way?"

"No," her dad replied. "But they change frequently, right?" Lou Lou sighed and looked out the window at the colors streaking past. It was clear that her dad didn't have any helpful information. Adults can be so unobservant sometimes, she thought. Lou Lou hoped that she would never be so grown-up that she wouldn't pay attention to the little details.

"Here we are!" Lou Lou's dad exclaimed as he stopped the car in front of You're Crafty Crafts. Inside, Lou Lou wasted no time filling a basket with ribbon, construction paper, and tassels. She added fake cobwebs, Silly String, and hanging paper phantoms for the ghost ship. Her final item was plucked from a bucket of brilliant-hued peacock feathers. Lou Lou chose the loveliest of all for her best friend.

She headed toward the cash register where her dad was chatting with the cashier. But someone beat her to it. That someone was a boy with spiky blue hair and a studded leather bracelet on his left wrist.

Lou Lou gasped and ducked back behind an aisle,

her ears blending in with a display of red colored pencils. What is *he* doing here? she thought, as Jeremy put his basket on the counter. He began to take out items— first paintbrushes, then tubes of paint in various colors, including rose reds, lemon yellows, emerald greens, midnight blacks, plum purples and, of course, peacock blues.

"Mural paint! Is *he* changing the murals?" Lou Lou wondered, not realizing she was wondering aloud until Jeremy paused and looked around. Lou Lou ducked back behind the aisle, nearly toppling the pencil display. She clamped her hand over her mouth so not another sound would come out.

After what seemed like an eternity, Jeremy took his change and walked to the door. As he was leaving, she noticed a white spot on the knee of his black jeans.

"Bleach!" Lou Lou said aloud despite herself, remembering Pinky's planticide. Luckily, her hand was still covering her mouth so it sounded like a muffled, "Bleeeet." When Jeremy was finally gone, Lou Lou scurried out from her hiding place.

"Okay, Dad! I'm ready. Let's pay and leave!" If they hurried, Lou Lou thought they might see Jeremy on the ride home, and she could determine what other mischief he was up to.

"Sure thing," her dad said as the cashier slowly put Lou Lou's supplies into a bag. Another eternity passed before they were in the car and pulling out of the parking lot. But instead of turning toward the SS *Lucky Alley* and Jeremy's likely route, Lou Lou's dad drove in the opposite direction.

"Where are we going?!" squealed Lou Lou.

"Groceries, don't you remember?" her dad answered. "It's buccaneer baked potato night and I need potatoes!"

"Right," said Lou Lou, slouching down and looking glumly out the window. She was disappointed that she wouldn't get to follow Jeremy to see if he was the mysterious mural painter. But Lou Lou knew one thing for certain—if he was, she was definitely going to find out.

CHAPTER TEN
A Very Bad Monday for Danielle Desserts

It was the Monday after Pinky's planticide, and Lou Lou was in Science class barely paying attention. She had way more important things to think about—Pinky, of course; Día de los Muertos; the changing murals; and Jeremy, who was being his suspicious self somewhere in Lou Lou's *very own* school. A sharp voice interrupted Lou Lou's thoughts.

"Louise Bombay, I asked you a question. Come back to reality, please!" The science teacher, Miss Mash, looked sternly at Lou Lou. Miss Mash had gray hair pulled into a bun and thin, pursed lips. She had a particular love of taupe. Everything she wore was taupe, like the color of a paper bag bleached by the sun.

"Please, Miss Mash, it's Lou Lou, not Louise." Lou Lou knew this was a lost cause. Most of her teachers used Lou Lou's preferred nickname, but not Miss Mash. Whether she refused to do so or just didn't remember, Lou Lou couldn't be sure. But her bets were on stubborn refusal.

"My question wasn't about your name," said Miss Mash, looming over Lou Lou so that all she could see was taupe. "I asked you to tell me why water is important to our ecosystem." Miss Mash used props in her lessons so she was holding a glass beaker filled almost to the brim with water.

"Yeah, answer the question, Lou Lou Loser," said a high-pitched voice behind Lou Lou, followed by a chorus of giggles. Lou Lou felt her ears tingle. She spun around in her seat to glare at her nemesis, Danielle Desserts.

Lou Lou had known Danielle since first grade, but they had never been friends. Danielle was a snob who pranced down the hall tossing her hair and rolling her eyes at people who dared speak to her. She thought she was more grown-up than everyone else just because she was the eldest in their class by three days and wore lip gloss and pink shoes with little heels. It wasn't as if Lou Lou had anything against lip gloss, and she loved her own hot pink sneakers—it was Danielle's attitude that was the problem. And the truth was that whiny Danielle was one of the most immature people Lou Lou knew.

The real trouble between Danielle and Lou Lou started in third grade when they were both finalists in the school's creative writing contest. Danielle wrote about the Sugar Mountain Sisters, Shelly and Sherry, two girls from her favorite books. When Lou Lou won the contest with her story about a talking fern, Danielle was furious. Lou Lou figured she was just jealous, but her jealousy turned into meanness.

"You probably think water is important because your stupid fern wants to make stupid tea," Danielle said now.

Lou Lou mostly ignored Danielle Desserts and her snooty-girl posse. But after Pinky's planticide, Lou Lou was in no mood for teasing. She skipped her *chrysanthemums* and turned to face her nemesis.

"Really, Danielle? Another fern insult?" Lou Lou gave her a hard look. "I'm sorry you didn't win a prize. Your story was good, but it's been a couple years now, and I think you need to get over it."

Danielle scrunched up her face and Lou Lou knew she'd struck a nerve.

"Lou Lou Bombay, you're just—just—just *stupid!*" shrieked Danielle. She'd never been good with insults. "The Sugar Mountain Sisters are just—just—just *perfect!*" Danielle wasn't good with compliments either. "And so was my story," she said, leaping from her seat to better glare at Lou Lou.

"Girls! Danielle! Louise! Stop this!" Miss Mash waved her arms. She'd clearly forgotten she was holding the beaker of water that started the whole problem. Lou Lou watched the water swishing back and forth, dangerously close to spilling over the edge.

"I've had enough chatter from you both!" Miss Mash flung her arm in Danielle's direction and the entire contents of the beaker flew into the air and soaked Danielle Desserts.

Danielle screamed. She was a sopping-wet mass of blond hair and Sugar Mountain Sisters bows. Miss Mash looked shocked. Lou Lou tried not to laugh.

"Go to the principal's office, both of you! *Now!*" shouted Miss Mash.

A furious Danielle spun around, her soaked hair spraying water on her snooty-girl posse. Lou Lou followed, but Danielle slammed the classroom door behind her. Lou Lou reopened it gently and stepped into the hallway.

Out of Miss Mash's sight, she finally laughed. Even as the possibility of getting her first detention made her ears burn, Lou Lou couldn't help thinking that the look on Danielle's dripping face had made it all worth it. And she couldn't wait to tell Pea.

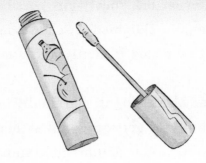

CHAPTER ELEVEN
Danielle Desserts's Day Gets Worse

Clomp, clomp, clomp! Danielle stomped down the hallway as best she could in her heels. Lou Lou followed at a safe distance, zigzagging around Danielle's wet trail. When they arrived at Principal Garcia's office, he looked up from a stack of papers.

"I'm not sure I want to know what happened. Something tells me that you didn't go on a field trip to swim in the bay, Danielle," said Principal Garcia, shooing her away from sitting in one of his desk chairs. "Jeepers. You'll stain the leather."

Principal Garcia frowned at Lou Lou and she got the hint she wasn't welcome to sit either.

"And you, Lou Lou," said Principal Garcia sternly. "What do you have to do with this fiasco?" Before Lou Lou could answer, she heard a loud throat-clearing noise.

"I will give you the official report," Kyle Longfellow said in his Comet Cop voice. He'd been sent to explain the situation. "Miss Mash was holding water and then Danielle said something to Lou Lou about a fern and then Lou Lou said, 'Get over it,' and then Miss Mash got Danielle wet and then—"

"Okay, okay." Principal Garcia held up his hands to cut Kyle off. Kyle's statements always sounded more like tattles than official reports. "This certainly is a mess. But it seems like it was an accident," said Principal Garcia. He looked at Lou Lou a little less sternly. In fact, Lou Lou could tell he was trying not to smile under his bushy mustache. That's probably why he has that mustache, Lou Lou thought. It was a good disguise for when he was laughing at the wrong time.

"You girls should try to be nicer to each other," said Principal Garcia. Danielle rolled her eyes and pouted.

"But since this doesn't seem to be either one of your faults, and neither of you make much trouble for me, I will let you off with a warning. Danielle, do you have gym clothes in your locker?" Danielle paled at this question, horrified by the thought of wearing gym clothes outside of Gym. But she nodded yes.

"Okay, then. Shoo and dry off." Principal Garcia waved the unwelcome guests out of his office. "Lou Lou, you go with Danielle and help her. Find her a towel or something. Maybe try to become friends. Kyle, you, too. Make sure they stay out of trouble."

Once again, Lou Lou found herself following Danielle down the hall, this time to Danielle's locker, with Kyle tagging along at the rear and talking to his two offenders.

"No funny business, guys. You know I'm in charge of these halls. Principal Garcia even said so. Well, sort of. He said I could be a hall monitor with no special privileges, but you know what that means, right?" Both Danielle and Lou Lou were ignoring him.

Danielle's locker was decorated with glittery stickers that said *Shelly Rules! Sherry Is Cool!* and *I Heart Sugar Mountain!* Danielle worked the lock, glancing suspiciously at Lou Lou and Kyle to make sure they weren't trying to memorize her combination. How ridiculous, thought Lou Lou. She would never steal, and certainly not whatever Danielle kept in her locker.

"Would you get a move on, Danielle?" said Kyle. "It's

almost lunch period. And it's spaghetti day so I need to get there on time."

Danielle began to rummage through her locker more slowly to annoy Kyle. Finally, she pulled out pink sweatpants with *Sweet* spelled out in shiny letters along the leg, and a matching T-shirt.

Lou Lou turned to walk away, as she supposed her work "helping" Danielle was done. She liked spaghetti day, too, and the best meatballs were claimed early. Lou Lou had only taken one step when she heard *thunk, thunk, clatter, clatter*. She turned around to find Danielle throwing things out of her locker. She'd tossed out all her books (the *thunk*s) and had moved on to school supplies like pencil holders and staplers (the *clatter*s). Lou Lou narrowly dodged a flying box of markers.

"What are you doing, Danielle?" Lou Lou exclaimed. "Can't you just change quietly so we can all get some spaghetti without getting into more trouble?" Danielle didn't answer. She made high-pitched noises of frustration as she furiously riffled through her locker. Danielle dumped out the entire contents of her purse, and Lou Lou resisted the urge to crunch a cherry-cola lip gloss with her shoe.

"C'mon, Danielle!" said Kyle impatiently.

"I lost it! It's gone!" Danielle threw up her hands and flopped down onto her knees. She looked as if she might cry.

Lou Lou was curious. "Lost what?"

"My best-friends shining-star necklace!" Danielle pointed to a photo of herself and her friends, taped to the inside of her locker. Lou Lou looked closely.

"You mean the pink necklace with four stars?" she asked. Each girl in the photo wore the same one. "That's what you lost?"

"It's not pink! It's rose gold! Because 'Best friends are as pretty as roses and as precious as gold'!" Danielle shrieked. The necklace seemed to have been inspired by the Sugar Mountain Sisters, Shelly and Sherry. Lou Lou wanted to roll her eyes, but Danielle's mention of best friends reminded her of Pea.

"It was in its special pocket in my purse," Danielle went on. "I wasn't wearing it today because it's raining and I have Gym later and I didn't want it to get dirty or broken or wet." She looked down at her soaked sweater in disgust. "But it's not there! It's not in my locker! It's not anywhere!" Danielle put her face in her hands and started to cry.

For once, Lou Lou felt bad for her sworn enemy. She seemed so pathetic—wet and crying on the floor over her jewelry. Lou Lou could sympathize, as she had with Magdalena, about losing something impor-tant. She thought of Pinky and bit her lip so it wouldn't tremble.

Lou Lou reached out to pat Danielle's shoulder. But

then Danielle looked up at Lou Lou. Her cheeks were streaked with tears and her eyes were filled with rage.

"*You!* You took it, didn't you, Lou Lou Bombay? Admit it! You've always been jealous of me!" Danielle was practically screaming.

"*Chrysanthemum, chrysanthemum, chrysanthemum,*" Lou Lou said under her breath. She tried not to get mad, and instead remember that Danielle was only upset because her special necklace was missing. "Listen, Danielle, I swear I did not take your necklace. In fact, I swear it on my third-grade writing contest trophy," said Lou Lou. "If you find out I'm lying, I will give you the trophy and tell everyone that you're the real winner, okay?" Danielle looked less angry.

"I'll even help you look for it," Lou Lou offered. She turned to enlist Kyle in the search, but he had trudged off, dreaming of spaghetti. Some interplanetary police officer he'll be, Lou Lou thought. She knelt down to sort through the mess on the floor.

After ten minutes spent going through Danielle's purse two more times, shaking out spiral-bound notebooks, and emptying makeup bags, it was clear they weren't going to find the best-friends shining-star necklace.

"Could you have left it somewhere?" Lou Lou asked. "At home maybe?"

"No! I always keep it in my purse. It was definitely stolen!" She started to cry again. Then, without a word of thanks to Lou Lou, Danielle clomped off to the bathroom to change.

CHAPTER TWELVE
Sugar Skulls

After the Danielle Desserts excitement, the remainder of the school day dragged on. Lou Lou slogged through Music and Social Studies and even had trouble paying attention in English, her favorite class. Finally, the last bell rang. Lou Lou rushed out the front door, barely noticing the rain. This was no ordinary Monday afternoon filled with snacks and homework. She had different plans.

Instead of catching the bus back to the SS *Lucky Alley*, she was going with Pea to decorate sugar skulls. Lou Lou opened the door of the sky-blue car that was waiting for her in front of her school.

"Hi!" she said to Henry Pearl, as she slid in next to her best friend. "Thanks for coming to pick me up today!"

"Hello there, Lou Lou. You are very welcome," replied the dapper man in the navy suit. Pea wasn't the only member of the Pearl family who liked blue.

"Hola, mi amigo," Lou Lou said to Pea. "Tú te ves muy bonito hoy." Pea was dressed in her school uniform with an aqua scarf around her neck and her hair coiled in braids.

"*Amiga* and *bonita*," Pea noted. "Because I am a girl. But you were close. Muy bien. And gracias for saying I look pretty."

During the short ride to the corner of Twenty-First Street, Lou Lou told Pea about Danielle Desserts. Pea was amused by wet Danielle but frowned when Lou Lou mentioned the missing jewelry.

"Maybe she just misplaced—" Pea began.

"No way. I think it was stolen," interrupted Lou Lou. "She swore she always keeps it in her special purse pocket. It seemed really important to her so I doubt she just lost it."

"Here we are." Pea's father pulled to the curb in front of a red building with a sign that read: SARAH'S STUDIO. "I will call your parents, Lou Lou, to let them know

I dropped you off safely. Be back at Lou Lou's by five, girls." Pea nodded and gave her father a hug.

"Thanks again, Henry!" Lou Lou said. She put her arm through Pea's and ducked under her umbrella to get out of the rain. She felt a surge of excitement. It was time for sugar skulls!

Sugar skulls, or calaveras, were a Día de los Muertos arts and crafts tradition. Sugar was molded into a skull shape the size of a grapefruit and set aside to harden. Once the skull was firm, it was ready for decorating. Paint, glitter, gems, buttons, fabric, pipe cleaners, toothpicks . . . There were many design choices. Some decorators would create sugar skulls that looked like animals or people, with a name written on the forehead or a headdress of flowers. Other skulls were just adorned with a colorful hodgepodge of odds and ends. The possibilities were unlimited.

Lou Lou and Pea entered the studio, a warmly lit room filled with long tables. Bright tapestries adorned the brick walls and multicolored vases of marigolds sat on each table. Sarah's Studio was home to many of El Corazón's community arts and crafts. Lou Lou and Pea had visited to paint colorful Mexican Talavera-style pottery, make batik scarves, and craft Fourth of July decorations. Today, designers of all ages were hard at work on their sugar skull masterpieces. Pea waved to two of Magdalena's friends.

"¡Hola, Zoe y Sofia!"

"Hi, Peacock!"

In one corner, a woman with red hair and dark-brown-rimmed glasses was sorting through a basket of beads. She smiled when she saw Lou Lou and Pea.

"Bienvenidas, Lou Lou Bombay and Peacock Pearl! I was hoping you would come today." The woman was Sugar Skulls Sarah. Or at least that was what Lou Lou and Pea called her. Her name was really just Sarah, but as a genius who molded all the sugar skulls herself, then helped everyone with their decorations, she'd earned her nickname.

"¡Buenas tardes, Sugar Skulls Sarah!" said Pea.

"Yes, yes! ¡Buenas tardes!" echoed Lou Lou.

Sarah handed each of them a bare sugar skull. "I saved some goodies just for you two." She held out a bowl of shiny sequins, brightly colored feathers, and other treasures. Lou Lou and Pea sat down at the end of a table dusted with gold glitter from the previous artists. Lou Lou sorted through the bowl, picking out anything close to magenta.

"I'm doing a tribute to Pinky to go along with the altar," she said, arranging small pinkish-purple jewels in a flower shape on the top of her skull.

"Great idea," replied Pea, busy fastening feathers at various angles. Pea always chose an artful blue-and-green peacock theme for her sugar skull.

They worked quietly for a while, listening to their fellow decorators' chatter. The room was cozy against the backdrop of the gray rainy day, and Lou Lou was relaxed, a rare feeling for her since Pinky's planticide. She painted petals on her skull and thought of her autumn queen camellia.

Lou Lou's calm focus was broken when the door chimed. She glanced up, expecting to see one of her classmates or another neighborhood friend. Instead, to Lou Lou's surprise, Jeremy strode into the studio. He grinned when Sugar Skulls Sarah handed him a skull, then took a seat at one of the tables.

"Pea," Lou Lou whispered urgently, feeling her ears prickle with heat.

"What?" Pea concentrated on applying glue to a blue gem.

"That's him." Lou Lou jerked her head at Jeremy.

"Who?" asked Pea, still not looking up.

"Jeremy!" Lou Lou hissed too loudly. He looked

directly at Lou Lou. She quickly glanced away but it was too late. She'd been spotted.

"Hey there!" called Jeremy from the other end of the table.

Lou Lou knew ignoring him would be useless so she waved halfheartedly. "Hi."

"How's it going, neighbor?" asked Jeremy.

"Okay." Lou Lou hoped this would be the end of their conversation, but Jeremy strode over to Lou Lou and Pea.

"Lou Lou, right?" Jeremy asked.

"Mm-hmm." She didn't try to return his friendliness. And Jeremy seemed not to care.

"Hiya," he said to Pea. "I'm Jeremy." He reached out his hand to Pea, and Lou Lou looked for streaks of mural paint. There were none, but she noticed that his fingernails were caked with dirt and there were smudges of mud on his wrist.

"Why are your hands so dirty?" Lou Lou asked.

"Dirty?" Jeremy tried to sound innocent. "Oh, I hadn't really noticed. Must be grease from helping my uncle fix his bike."

"Um, okay." Lou Lou wasn't convinced. She knew the difference between grease and soil, and the spots on Jeremy's hands definitely looked like soil.

"Like I was saying, I'm Jeremy. And you are . . . ?" he asked Pea. Pea accepted his outstretched hand but let go after one quick shake. Lou Lou saw her wipe her fingers on her handkerchief under the table.

"Peacock Pearl, Lou Lou's best friend. Very nice to meet you." Pea couldn't help but be polite. "I like the color of your hair," she added.

"Gracias and nice to meetcha, too," Jeremy replied, sounding fake friendly. And his ear-to-ear smile seemed too big to be real. He's overdoing it so we won't suspect he's a criminal, Lou Lou thought.

"Is there any rhyme to your reason?" Jeremy was speaking to Lou Lou now. She was confused until he pointed at her sugar skull.

"It's a tribute," Lou Lou replied warily. It was difficult to talk about the crime and not accuse Jeremy outright. But she needed proof that he was behind Pinky's death so she didn't want him to know about her suspicions. At least not yet.

"It's a tribute to Pinky, my autumn queen camellia." Lou Lou took a deep breath and said, "Pinky would have won the Hello Horticulture! Society Flowering Bushes and Shrubs blue ribbon this year, if someone hadn't committed a planticide last weekend." She waited for Jeremy's reaction. His eyes widened slightly, and he put his hands behind his back as if to hide the dirty evidence. But when he spoke, he sounded casual and relaxed.

"A planticide, huh? Bummer."

"Maybe you saw something from your yard?" asked Pea. "Like who did it or what happened?"

"Nope," replied Jeremy. "Wish I could be more helpful." He turned to walk away, then looked back and asked, "Any suspects?"

"A few," said Lou Lou, certain she was looking right at the prime suspect. "You can be sure we'll figure it out."

"Yes," added Pea. "You can count on it."

"Okay, good luck. I hope it's not a tough mystery to solve." Jeremy went back to his sugar skull.

Lou Lou waited until he was immersed in his artwork and then leaned in to whisper to Pea. "He did it! He must have, don't you think? *I hope it's not a tough mystery to solve*," Lou Lou mimicked Jeremy. "He's taunting us! He doesn't want us to solve it! You saw the dirt on his hands. It looks like he's been in a garden. *My* garden. Killing Pinky!" Lou Lou whispered. Her ears felt like little flames.

"You really think he hasn't washed his hands since

Saturday?" Pea sounded horrified. Lou Lou ignored the question.

"And the paint, Pea! I told you I saw him at the crafts store buying *mural* colors. I know he's up to something with the murals, too. I bet he painted Helado and Magdalena's dress!"

"How would he know about Magdalena's dress?" Pea asked.

"He'd know if he's behind the crime. He is probably the grape-juice-and-dye villain!" replied Lou Lou.

Pea considered this. "Isn't it possible he's just painting something else? Maybe a portrait of a friend or a pet?" she asked. Pea had painted many portraits of Lou Lou, Uno, and Dos in different settings and costumes. "Why would he commit crimes and then paint them? And why would he kill Pinky?"

"I don't know yet," Lou Lou admitted. "But we'll find out!"

"We can keep an eye on him," said Pea. "We have a good view from your window so we can see if he does anything suspicious."

"Definitely!" Lou Lou replied. "Can you sleep over this weekend?"

"I will have to ask my parents. But probably."

"It seems like so much bad stuff has happened to people in the last week. Magdalena, Pinky, Danielle Desserts . . ." Lou Lou said.

"It is sad." Pea shook her head. "I hate to see troubles come to our neighborhood."

"That's exactly why we need to figure out what's going on!" said Lou Lou.

Pea nodded and went back to work on her sugar skull. Lou Lou tried to concentrate, but her mind was spinning. Pea was right about Jeremy. He didn't have an obvious reason to hurt Pinky. It was possible he was just cruel, but Lou Lou felt it was something more. Maybe he had a grudge against camellias? Maybe he traveled around poisoning people's plants? Maybe the crime was part of an initiation into some secret society like the kind she'd read about in books?

Lou Lou pondered the possibilities until she realized she had been neglecting her sugar skull, and Pea was putting the finishing touches on hers. Lou Lou quickly added the final details to her masterpiece.

"Marvelous," said Pea when Lou Lou finished the last petal and presented her creation for Pea's approval. Nearly every inch of the surface was covered in flowers made from beads and small buttons. For the sugar skull's eyes, Lou Lou used green plastic gems that sparkled as she turned it around. "Pinky would be proud."

"Yours looks fantastic too, Pea," Lou Lou said, examining Pea's blue-and-green sugar skull. It was skillfully covered with green pipe cleaner spirals and bright blue feathers.

"For now. Until Uno and Dos get their paws on it." Lou Lou laughed. Pea's cats loved anything sweet, which Pea had discovered when she found a bag of jelly beans almost entirely devoured. The candy had made Uno and Dos sick, and Pea spent an hour cleaning their rainbow vomit off her carpet. Last year she'd caught them licking her sugar skull when they thought she wasn't looking.

"I almost forgot." Lou Lou handed Pea the beautiful peacock feather she had bought at the crafts store.

"Thank you!" Pea stuck the feather into the top of her skull as an elegant headdress.

It was time to go. Lou Lou and Pea gently placed their sugar skulls in plastic bags so they wouldn't melt in the rain. They headed for the door, trying to slip by Jeremy unnoticed. It seemed they were going to be successful until Sugar Skulls Sarah called out, "Lou Lou Bombay and Peacock Pearl! You weren't going to leave without saying goodbye, were you?"

Jeremy turned around in his chair. Lou Lou was standing directly behind him. "Yeah, you weren't going to leave without saying goodbye? That's not very neighborly." He blinked at Lou Lou.

"Goodbye!" she said curtly. Then she noticed Jeremy's sugar skull. Lou Lou stepped back in surprise, nearly crashing into Pea.

Jeremy had decorated the skull almost entirely in white, using short white downy feathers to give it a furry look. Whiskers were made from white pipe cleaners. But it was the skull's eyes, amber-colored glass gems, that really caught Lou Lou's attention. The resemblance was unmistakable—Helado. From the look on Pea's face, Lou Lou knew she was thinking the same thing.

"Cool sugar skull, Jeremy. What gave you the idea for that?" Lou Lou tried to copy Jeremy's casual tone despite her shock.

"I guess I've always wanted a pet rabbit." Jeremy grinned.

"Okay, we really have to go now!" Lou Lou pulled the hood of her rain jacket over her head, turned on her heel, and was out the door before Pea even managed her first step.

CHAPTER THIRTEEN
Seeing Stars and Finding Flowers

Outside the studio, Lou Lou and Pea huddled together to escape the rain and talk in secret as they walked.

"See! He knows about Helado!" Lou Lou said. "I'd bet you five cupcakes something bad happened to that bunny. That's why Helado is in a mural, just like Magdalena's dress!"

"You're right, he probably does know," said Pea. "White bunnies with amber eyes are not exactly popping up around the neighborhood every day like tabby cats and black Labradors."

"This stuff has to be related, and Jeremy must be

behind it all!" replied Lou Lou. "He did something to Helado, ruined Magdalena's dress, and killed Pinky. I just know it! He probably stole Danielle's necklace, too."

"But there's no connection between Jeremy and Danielle or Magdalena—"

"No connection that we know of *yet*," Lou Lou interrupted. "We need to put all the pieces together and stop these crimes so no one else gets hurt!"

They continued walking the short distance to the SS *Lucky Alley* in the rain. The sky was dark with clouds and the street lamps came on early, bathing sections of their route in pools of light. Halloween decorations were up all over the neighborhood and witches on broomsticks cackled silently, while plastic-bag ghosts swayed in trees. Lou Lou watched flickers of orange through the eyes of a spooky jack-o'-lantern. If it could speak, she thought, it would be saying, *Trouble is a-brewing, Lou Lou Bombay.*

Suddenly, Pea gasped and stopped.

"What is it?" asked Lou Lou. She followed Pea's gaze to the last house on their left. A mural, partially illuminated by a streetlight, covered the doorway and the front wall. *A Lovely Day for a Parade* showed a festive spectacle of children prancing with balloons and women carrying baskets of fruit. People leaned out of windows waving blue-and-yellow flags. Lou Lou scanned the mural to see what had caught Pea's eye.

"Look," said Pea. "That woman's basket had peaches in it before." Here was Lou Lou's turn to gasp. The peaches were gone and the basket was now painted full of brownish-green leaves, branches, and shriveling flowers. Not just any flowers, but magenta autumn queen camellia blooms.

"Pinky!" Lou Lou cried. "Pinky is in the mural!"

"There's something else!" Pea exclaimed. She was looking at another mural on the next building. Lou Lou and Pea called this one *Dancing in Space* because rings of dancers frolicked on different planets in the solar system. A circle of people twirled and kicked up their legs on Earth, a group of white-and-black dogs danced paw to paw on Mars, turtles sashayed around Saturn's rings, and kangaroos pranced on Venus. The space above the dancers had been a blank expanse of black. But now there were four huge rose-gold stars in a row linked with a painted chain. It only took Lou Lou a second to tie the stars to the day's events.

"Danielle Desserts! That's her best-friends shining-star necklace," Lou Lou said. "I knew it! Helado,

Magdalena, Pinky, and even Danielle Desserts are for sure connected. It's mural mischief. No, it's a Mural Mystery. And Jeremy must be the culprit!"

"But other people know about Pinky's planticide and could have changed the mural, right?" Pea asked. "I'm not saying it's *not* Jeremy, just that we should keep an open mind. Who else did you tell about the planticide? And who knows about Danielle's necklace? We need a complete list of suspects before we can be certain about anything."

Lou Lou counted off the people she'd told about Pinky's death. Besides Jeremy, there were her parents and Pea, but naturally they could be eliminated as suspects. Then there was Juan at Green Thumb, everyone who worked at Cupcake Cabana, Elmira, Magdalena, the mail lady, Lou Lou's English class, the old man who fed the ducks in Limonero Park, Lou Lou's bus driver . . . The list was long, and Lou Lou was sure she was forgetting people. As for Danielle's best-friends shining-star necklace, everyone at school knew it had gone missing. Danielle had complained and cried about it all afternoon.

"I guess it could have been someone else," Lou Lou said. Pea was right—she couldn't *completely* rule out other people. "What do you think the murals mean and why is Jeremy—I mean, *someone* from our list of suspects—changing them? Is the villain just bragging about his own crimes?" She looked at Pinky's withered painted image again and felt a pang of sadness.

"I don't know. It doesn't make sense. Most criminals would want to keep their crimes a secret," Pea replied. They thought about this silently for a moment. "We better get going, Lou Lou. It's almost five o'clock," added Pea.

"Okay," said Lou Lou reluctantly. She wanted to examine the murals more carefully, but Henry Pearl was due at the SS *Lucky Alley* and Lou Lou couldn't miss her dad's famous landlubber lasagna. She took one last look at the painted camellia and vowed to herself that they would solve the Mural Mystery. They'd find the person who had killed poor Pinky and stolen Lou Lou's blue-ribbon dreams.

CHAPTER FOURTEEN
A Surprise Encounter at the Candle Shop

After the incident in Miss Mash's class, Lou Lou knew she had to avoid any more trouble at school that week. She had a lot to do before Día de los Muertos and she couldn't risk detention. Lou Lou worked extra hard on her deadly nightshade Halloween story for English, aced her History test, and even volunteered to stay late to help first graders make paper jack-o'-lanterns.

On Thursday after school, Lou Lou planned to go to *A Lovely Day for a Parade* and *Dancing in Space* to take a closer look at the mural changes. But when she was rushing to her bus someone blocked her way.

"Let me by, Kyle," Lou Lou huffed.

"Stop running in the halls, Lou Lou Bombay," Kyle commanded. His voice came out squeaky. "It's against the rules. I'll arrest you and take you to see Principal Garcia."

"You wish," replied Lou Lou. "Now move, please."

"Watch it or I'll get you in trouble and then you'll be painted into a detention mural."

Lou Lou stopped pushing and looked hard at Kyle.

"There is no detention mural, Kyle. And what do you know about the murals, anyway? Have you seen the changes? Are *you* the one changing them?"

"No, not me," Kyle said, taking a step back.

"Do you know who is?"

"No," Kyle said again. "I just know they're changing in a funny way. Most people don't pay attention to the details, but I have laser-beam eyes like Comet Cop." Kyle pointed to his face with two fingers to illustrate his point.

Lou Lou relaxed a little. "Pea and I think the murals are connected to crimes that have been happening around here." Lou Lou was certain that the mention of crimes would make Comet Cop Kyle interested.

"Criminal activity, huh? Well, if it's important to Peacock—I mean, to the earthlings I am sworn to protect—then I will keep my laser-beam eyes and supersonic ears open." Kyle patted his pocket. "Now where did I put my force-field penetrator?"

Lou Lou, seeing her chance, finally managed to pass Kyle as he searched for his missing space gear. "See you later, Kyle!"

"I'm feeling generous today so I will let you off with a warning!" Kyle called after her.

Lou Lou narrowly avoided missing her bus and, after a brief stop at the SS *Lucky Alley* to drop off her bag and get her parents' permission to go for a walk, she finally made it to *A Lovely Day for a Parade* and *Dancing in Space*. Pinky and Danielle Desserts's necklace were still there. Lou Lou looked closely at the details, but found nothing else to help her with the Mural Mystery and left frustrated. She had a little time before she needed to be home so she decided to go to Cupcake Cabana, thinking that vanilla buttercream would lift her spirits.

Halfway to the bakery, Lou Lou changed her mind and turned toward the candle shop instead. She needed answers, not frosting. And she hoped Elmira could give her guidance.

When Lou Lou arrived at the candle shop, Elmira

saw her through the window. The Candle Lady flashed a smile and waved Lou Lou inside.

"Buenas tardes, Lou Lou Bombay."

"Hola, Elmira." As Lou Lou's eyes adjusted to the dim candlelight, she realized they were not alone. Danielle Desserts was at the counter, putting her sparkly wallet into her pink purse. Lou Lou scowled. She didn't want Danielle to intrude on her Candle Lady time.

"Danielle dropped in for some assistance," Elmira explained, clearly seeing the sour look on Lou Lou's face. "She seems to be experiencing a nagging necklace nightmare and needs a 'find' candle to ensure that she gets her missing jewelry back."

Danielle glanced at Lou Lou, rolled her eyes once, and half stuck out her tongue. But Lou Lou sensed that Danielle's heart wasn't in it. Danielle had been ignoring Lou Lou at school since Monday's events, which was a big step up from her usual taunting. If Danielle appreciated Lou Lou's help with the necklace search, she clearly wasn't about to admit it.

Danielle Desserts flounced toward the door, holding an orange candle with a picture of a magnifying glass and the word *Encontrar* on the glass holder. She pushed by Lou Lou, tossing her hair. "Move it, Bombay," she said. Then quietly, "Please."

Lou Lou was shocked. She had never heard Danielle say *please* before. When the bell on the door signaled Danielle's exit, Lou Lou turned to Elmira.

"Does Danielle come here often?" she asked. Despite Danielle's slightly improved attitude, Lou Lou didn't want Danielle around during her future candle shop visits.

"A veces," Elmira replied. "She was just here the other day to buy a Victoria candle so she could win tickets to the *Sugar Mountain* movie premiere."

"I see," said Lou Lou, trying not to giggle.

"Esa niña only visits when she needs help. She is not una buena amiga like you." Elmira smiled at Lou Lou. "How is your garden?" she asked. "Is the Crecer candle working to remedy your catastrophic camellia calamity?"

"It's not," said Lou Lou sadly. "But my toad lilies are doing great, and I have more basil than ever. I guess maybe it's working, just not for Pinky."

"I know you wanted to win that competition. But you are a skilled gardener who grows flores fabulosas. I'm sure there will be a blue ribbon in your future." Elmira reached across the counter and squeezed Lou Lou's hand.

"Thanks, Elmira!" Lou Lou felt a glimmer of hope. Elmira had cheered Lou Lou on during the third-grade writing contest and recommended a Creativo candle to get her literary juices flowing. And Lou Lou had won! So if Elmira said Lou Lou would win a horticulture blue ribbon someday, it must be true! Just not for Pinky. Thinking of her camellia, Lou Lou remembered the purpose of her visit.

"Elmira, do you know anything about the murals? Someone is adding things to them that weren't there before. Real-life bad things, too."

The Candle Lady raised her eyebrows. "I wasn't aware of any changes, but ya entiendo. Mysterious mural mayhem is your problem."

"Exactly, Elmira! It's a Mural Mystery! Danielle's missing necklace was in a mural. Magdalena's quinceañera dress was painted, too. And there's a bunny! A white bunny with amber eyes. I'm not sure what that means since I don't know any white bunnies in the neighborhood. But I think the same person is behind all these crimes and he is—I mean, he *or* she—is using the murals to brag. I have to put a stop to it!" Lou Lou was building up steam. "And Pinky! Pinky is in *A Lovely Day for a Parade!*"

"Oh my," said Elmira. "It does sound like a puzzling painted picture. Let me see if I have something that can help you." She reached toward one of the shelves.

"I can't buy any candles today," Lou Lou said. "I don't get my allowance until tomorrow." Lou Lou only had one dollar and four quarters ("one cupcake") in her pocket. "But I thought you might know something useful."

"It pains me that so much misfortune has befallen our community recently." Elmira echoed Lou Lou and Pea's thoughts. "But it's possible that these murals are just meaningless paintings of sad events. Still, I will consider this confounding conundrum. Why don't you come back another time? I may have a better answer and, if not, you can get the right candle to illuminate the issue."

"Okay." Lou Lou was a little disappointed. But she knew that the Candle Lady cared about the people of El Corazón and would do her best to help with the Mural Mystery. "See you soon, Elmira."

"I hope so," replied Elmira. "I do enjoy your visits, Lou Lou Bombay."

"¡Adiós!" Lou Lou said to the Candle Lady, and left the shop.

When she arrived at the SS *Lucky Alley*, Lou Lou went straight to her garden. She winced at the sight of Pinky's remains. The pile of brown leaves, dried-up flower petals, and branches had been further destroyed by that week's rain. Lou Lou's mom had promised to clean up the mess tomorrow to spare Lou Lou the painful task. Then, on Saturday, which had been Lou Lou's favorite time to visit Pinky (and which she liked to think was Pinky's favorite time to visit Lou Lou), she would have a proper funeral befitting a would-have-been Hello Horticulture! Society Flowering Bushes and Shrubs blue-ribbon contender.

As she had done every day since Pinky's planticide, Lou Lou inspected her garden to make sure that there had been no more foul play. She saw no visible mischief so she knelt down to sniff the ground for poisons of the Pinky-killing variety. It was when she had her nose in the dirt that she heard a voice from the other side of the fence.

"Try not to worry," the voice said.

Jeremy! When Lou Lou opened her mouth to hiss his name, she got a mouthful of soil.

"Phhtt!" Lou Lou spit it out and Jeremy was quiet for a few long seconds. She froze, certain he would look over the fence any moment. Miraculously, he didn't.

"Of course I'm keeping it quiet. C'mon, you know me!" Jeremy said. Lou Lou couldn't hear another person so she assumed Jeremy was on the phone. "No, I don't think she's at all suspicious." Who? Me? Lou Lou almost laughed. Oh, I'm suspicious, she thought.

"¡Jeremy, es la hora de la cena!" Lou Lou heard a woman's voice call.

"Listen, I have to go. My mom is calling me for dinner. But I promise I'm handling it, okay?" Jeremy said.

He's probably working with another criminal! Lou Lou thought. Otherwise, why would he be talking to someone about being quiet and avoiding suspicion?

"Sí. ¡Mañana te llamo!" Jeremy said. Lou Lou heard her neighbor's door slam and she knew it was safe to stop kissing the dirt. She stood up, brushed herself off, and peeked over the fence. But all she saw were blue spikes in the window.

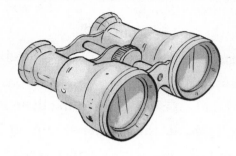

CHAPTER FIFTEEN
Rosa's Mascota

On Friday, Lou Lou could hardly wait to get back to the SS *Lucky Alley* after school. It was almost PSPP and she and Pea had big weekend plans. At home, Lou Lou went to her garden to wait for Pea. Of course Lou Lou felt sad about Pinky's absence, but she tried to focus on her toad lilies.

"You're looking lovely in polka dots today," she said to the flowers. Lou Lou peeked over the fence into her neighbor's yard but it was empty.

It wasn't long before Pea arrived with an overnight duffel slung over her shoulder. They quickly recited their traditional PSPP pleasantries so Lou Lou could tell Pea about Jeremy's phone conversation with his likely accomplice. Pea listened as she cut a perfect square of butter for her scone.

"It's unfortunate that we don't know the other half of that conversation," she said.

"I know," Lou Lou replied, dropping little strawberry spots on the table as she slathered jam on her scone. Pea wiped up the spots with a paper towel before Lou Lou had even noticed them.

"I brought my father's binoculars." Pea patted her duffel. "We can keep a close eye on your garden from the crow's nest window."

When she'd finished her scone, Pea began to take items from her duffel. She'd brought treasures for two of their weekend projects—making Pinky's altar and their procession outfits.

Pea pulled out the wooden frame with painted flowers they'd used for Bisabuela Nellie's altar. "Mmm, that will work for Pinky," said Lou Lou between mouthfuls of scone.

Then Pea held up a patchwork dress for her procession outfit. Lou Lou crinkled her nose as she considered it. "It's not my favorite but . . ." Pea chose something different.

"That one's perfect!" Lou Lou liked a long skirt that Pea had embroidered with multicolored butterflies.

"I like this better, too," Pea said.

"This is good for the top." Lou Lou sprayed scone crumbs as she pointed to a sapphire-blue sweater trimmed with black lace. After Pea finished her presentation and brushed off every last crumb, they went to retrieve Lou Lou's allowance. Her dad hid it in the pirate's treasure chest in a corner of the front hall. She rooted around in a mound of fake gold coins and jewels until she found it. The money was rolled up into a scroll tied with twine and wrapped in a note that read, *You're Greaty, Matey! Love, Dad.* Lou Lou giggled at his silliness.

"Mi padre es un sótano gracioso." She was proud of her complicated Spanish phrase. But Pea laughed.

"*Sótano* means cellar," Pea said. "You said, 'My father is a funny cellar.' I think maybe you mean *marinero*. That is the word for sailor."

"Oh, yeah," said Lou Lou. She'd get that one right next time. She pocketed the money, called her padre gracioso to tell him the plan for their PSPP stroll, and they were out the door a moment later.

Vanilla buttercream had won out over candles today, so Lou Lou and Pea went to Cupcake Cabana. They took a long route home to visit the murals and, on the way, they saw Rosa looking intently at *Lady Carmen Rides Bonito*. She didn't notice Lou Lou and Pea until they were close enough to count the rhinestones on her hair clip.

"Hi!" said Lou Lou. Rosa jumped and turned. She looked startled.

"It is very nice to see you again, Rosa," Pea said.

"Hola, Peacock and Lou Lou," Rosa said softly.

"Why are you staring at this mural?" Despite Lou Lou's good intentions, this sounded like an accusation. Pea's advice to be more sensitive came in the form of a gentle elbow to Lou Lou's ribs. "Sorry, I didn't mean to be rude. It's just that . . . maybe you've noticed the murals have been changing after bad things happen?" Lou Lou recounted the stories of Magdalena and Danielle Desserts and the tragedy of Pinky's planticide. Rosa nodded sympathetically as Lou Lou talked. Her eyes were misty and she wiped them with her sleeve.

"Yes, so many troubles . . ." Rosa trailed off as she looked back at the mural. Helado's amber eyes gazed back at her.

"Is Helado making you sad?" asked Lou Lou. Rosa seemed confused.

"The bunny," explained Pea. "He is new to the mural. We thought he needed a name so we picked Helado."

"Ice cream." Rosa smiled despite her tears. "I like that." She gazed at Helado. "The bunny you call Helado is mi mascota and my best friend. But I haven't seen him in two weeks. He has been bunnynapped!" Rosa whispered.

"How terrible!" exclaimed Pea.

"Have you called the police?" asked Lou Lou.

"No, no." Rosa shook her head. "I don't want to involve them in this."

That seemed odd to Lou Lou. "Rosa, do you have any idea who is behind the crimes and changing the murals?" she asked. "Is it Jeremy? Kid about our age, spiky blue hair, studded bracelet, black boots? Can't miss him."

Rosa looked at them strangely. Before she could reply, they heard the sound of fast-approaching footsteps around the corner.

"I'm sorry, I need to go." Rosa seemed nervous. "¡Hasta luego, Peacock and Lou Lou!" She hurried away, disappearing into someone's side yard.

"Why does she keep rushing off?" Pea wondered.

"I have no idea," Lou Lou said, and looked at the spot where Rosa had been. She had a feeling they'd been close to finding out something about the Mural Mystery. She turned toward the corner where the sound of footsteps had stopped.

Lou Lou caught a glimpse of a yellow bumblebee sweater as Kyle peered out, then quickly ducked back behind the corner.

"We see you, Kyle!" Lou Lou called. Kyle's head poked out again. He noticed Pea and emerged from his hiding spot.

"Where does a peacock go when it loses its tail?" Kyle asked, grinning. Lou Lou wondered how long he'd been waiting to tell this joke to Pea. "A retail store!" said Kyle. "Get it? *Re*-tail. As in, to get another tail."

"I get it," Pea replied, and Lou Lou couldn't help but laugh. It reminded her of one of Bisabuela Nellie's bad jokes. Encouraged, Kyle tried again.

"Wanna hear a space joke? I have a million of those."

"Why were you hiding just now, Kyle?" Lou Lou asked.

Kyle frowned. "I wasn't hiding. I was spying from my invisible spacecraft."

"Why are you so interested in us?" asked Lou Lou. Kyle's face turned red and he stole a glance at Pea.

"I'm not interested in *you guys*!" Kyle replied. "I'm keeping an eye out for anything suspicious in the neighborhood. Just like I told you I would, Lou Lou Bombay! Who was that girl looking at the mural? I've seen her around before but I don't know her."

"Her name is Rosa," said Pea. "She is very nice."

"I saw her yesterday, too," Kyle said. "She was talking to that new kid in our school. The one with blue hair and the studded wrist thingy."

Rosa and Jeremy! Lou Lou and Pea exchanged knowing looks.

"What were they talking about?" Pea asked.

"Dunno. I couldn't hear what they were saying, but she looked upset," Kyle said. "I was gonna tell him to stop bothering her, but he left before I got the chance.

He was probably scared off just looking at me since I'm so tough." Kyle pulled up his sleeve and flexed his biceps. Lou Lou smiled. She could fit one of her ponytail holders around his arm. "I was watching her today in case she needed my help," Kyle added.

Why was Rosa talking to Jeremy? Lou Lou wondered. He must have been threatening her. Maybe trying to get her to pay a bunny ransom for Helado's safe return. Which could explain Rosa's reluctance to get the police involved.

"Let's go." Lou Lou wanted to tell Pea about her ransom theory without Kyle Longfellow around.

"Goodbye, Kyle," Pea said, and turned.

"Wait! I should hang out with you guys. I can protect you with my supernova laser beam."

Lou Lou and Pea continued down the block. "Maybe next time!" Lou Lou called over her shoulder.

The sky was darkening and they had to head back to the SS *Lucky Alley*. As they walked and talked, Rosa's words echoed in Lou Lou's head.

So many troubles . . .

It's true, thought Lou Lou. And somehow the troubles have to stop!

CHAPTER SIXTEEN
Ella Divine Sings the Blues

At home, Lou Lou's dad was making shiver-me-timbers spaghetti and singing a sea shanty about mermaids of the deep. Lou Lou and Pea took plates to go and, dodging the Halloween phantoms hanging in the hall, went up to the crow's nest to eat and change for their night out. Lou Lou pulled on a silver satin dress while Pea debated choices from her duffel.

"The shimmery navy is my favorite but I wore it last time. I could wear the green sequined skirt instead and add some blue accents." Pea held up a headband and tights.

"Yeah, what you said sounds good." Lou Lou was peering out the window with Henry Pearl's binoculars. She focused on her asters, then on a patch of thyme in Eats and Cures. Nothing looked out of place.

"Which one? Shimmery navy or green sequins with blue accents?"

"What? Oh, sorry." Lou Lou looked at Pea. "Green sequins with blue accents. You wore the shimmery navy last time." Pea was polite enough not to point out she had just said that.

Ten minutes later, Lou Lou and Pea came down dressed in their stylish clothes.

"Don't you two look elegant," Lou Lou's dad remarked, straightening his tie. "Jane!" he called. "Time to go to the Heliotrope."

Every third Friday of the month, Lou Lou and Pea crossed their fingers that one or the other's parents would take them to the Heliotrope, a restaurant and theater a few blocks from the SS *Lucky Alley*. On these nights, Ella Divine performed her husky mix of blues and jazz. Lou Lou thought Ella Divine was the bee's knees when it came to singing, but it was Pea who truly adored the performer. Admiring her glamorous evening gowns, Pea always said she wanted to be like Ella Divine when she grew up. Except Pea would sing in

Spanish and wear blue, as well as Ella Divine's signature color, emerald green. Pea had already written her first song, "Me Encanta Limpiar Mi Habitación" ("I Love to Clean My Room").

After a short walk, Lou Lou and Pea were greeted by grand oak doors and the Heliotrope's lighted marquee, which read in big letters: *LIVE TONIGHT! THE LOVELY ELLA DIVINE!* And in smaller letters below: *Try our famous chocolate cheesecake!* Inside, Lou Lou's parents picked a table in the back and allowed Lou Lou and Pea to sit in a booth closer to the stage. The girls slid into the velvet-lined seat and Francesca, the waitress, waved from across the room. A few minutes later, Francesca brought over their usual: pomegranate Italian sodas topped with maraschino cherries and a piece of chocolate cheesecake with two forks.

"Thank you, Francesca," said Pea, taking a sip of her soda.

"Thanks!" echoed Lou Lou, stabbing a cherry with her straw.

"Y'all are very welcome," Francesca replied in her Southern drawl, which Lou Lou and Pea liked to imitate after nights at the Heliotrope.

As always, the show was packed with the singer's adoring fans. Pea waved to a girl from her school. Lou

Lou smiled at her music teacher and looked around for other familiar faces to greet. Just as the houselights went down, Lou Lou thought she spotted blue spikes at a table across the room. She squinted, but in the dark it was impossible to tell for certain if it was Jeremy.

"Pea! I think Jeremy's here!" Lou Lou whispered loudly.

Pea, who was eating chocolate cheesecake and watching the spotlight in anticipation, looked at Lou Lou.

"Where?"

Lou Lou pointed into the darkness. "Over there . . . somewhere . . ."

"I can't really see anything," said Pea.

"Shh!" A man in a neighboring booth hushed Lou Lou and Pea as Ella Divine emerged from behind the heavy crimson curtain. She looked beautiful in a lace emerald evening gown and shiny patent-leather pumps. Ella Divine's hair was curled and pinned into an elaborate hairstyle and her lips were painted a bright scarlet. She immediately launched into one of her most popular songs, "Feathered Fedora," which was Pea's favorite. The crowd cheered but Lou Lou frowned.

"She didn't say good evening like she always does," whispered Lou Lou. "Strange, right?"

"Mmm." Pea was engrossed in "Feathered Fedora."

Her eyes were half-closed and she was swaying to the music as she sang along softly:

> *"I am always where you're at.*
> *I'll be the feather in your hat.*
> *I'll be the flowers in your May.*
> *I'll be the sweet in your beignet."*

Suddenly, Pea snapped to attention as if waking from a dream. Instead of moving to the next verse of "Feathered Fedora," Ella Divine kept repeating the first lines.

"What's going on?" Lou Lou asked. Before Pea could reply, Ella Divine dropped her microphone. But the singing went on. The performer's eyes grew big, and she rushed offstage. The music stopped and the house-lights came on. Lou Lou's jaw dropped.

"Lip-synching?" gasped Lou Lou. "Ella Divine lip-synchs her songs?" Similar murmurs could be heard in the crowd. Ella Divine was known for her beautiful live performances. It was unthinkable that she was lip-synching.

People got up from their tables and booths to leave. All around outraged voices protested.

"Can you believe it? She's a fraud!"

"What a waste of money. I could have stayed home and listened to her album."

"The chocolate cheesecake may be good, but I am never coming here again!"

Lou Lou didn't see Jeremy in the angry crowd. Only Francesca, who was frantically trying to refill drinks so she wouldn't lose all her customers. Pea caught her eye as she dashed past their booth.

"What on earth, Francesca? Did you know that Ella Divine doesn't actually sing her songs during her performances?"

"But she usually does sing! I swear it!" said Francesca. "The lip-synching was just a onetime thing. Y'all have to believe me—she's not a fake."

"Can we go see her?" Lou Lou pointed backstage. They needed to talk to Ella Divine to find out what had happened.

Francesca hesitated, but gave in. "All right, go," she said. "Be quick about it. And don't get me in trouble by tellin' management that I sent you." Lou Lou glanced back at her parents' table. Her mom and dad were talking to a friend. Francesca followed her gaze.

"If they ask, I'll tell them I sent y'all back there," Francesca said. "Hurry up now."

Lou Lou and Pea checked that no one was watching,

then opened the small door near the stage, ignoring the sign that said: PERFORMERS AND EMPLOYEES ONLY / SÓLO ARTISTAS Y EMPLEADOS. They'd been backstage once before, on Pea's birthday, when Francesca took them to meet Ella Divine, so they knew exactly where to find the singer.

From outside the dressing room, Lou Lou and Pea could hear crying. Pea knocked lightly in the middle of the gold star that read: MISS DIVINE. Her idol opened the door a crack and peered out. Tears and mascara stained her cheeks, but she still looked beautiful.

"May I help you?" Ella Divine asked. Her voice was hoarse and scratchy. Lou Lou realized that they didn't have a plan for what to say.

Pea cleared her throat. "Miss Divine, my name is Peacock Pearl. I met you last year. You may not remember, but I do because I am your biggest fan. I come to your show every month with my friend here, Lou Lou Bombay."

"Nice to see you again," Lou Lou said, peeking around Pea's shoulder. Ella Divine managed a weak smile.

"Thank you," she said. "I do remember you. And of course I notice you at all my shows. You always look so fashionable." Lou Lou squeezed Pea's arm. She knew the compliment would mean a lot. "I hope you will keep coming, even after tonight," Ella Divine added. A tear spilled from the singer's eye. But she pulled herself together and graciously inquired, "Would you like an autograph? I think I have some photos from my days on the French Riviera. I could sign one for you."

"Actually, may we come in to talk to you?" Pea asked.

"I'm not very good company right now. But you two might be my only fans left." Ella Divine opened the door all the way to reveal her dressing room decked out with a chandelier, fancy emerald-green furniture, and patterned wallpaper. An Ave Cantora candle with a picture of a songbird on the glass holder burned in one corner next to a vase filled with lilies.

The singer motioned for them to sit, and Lou Lou and Pea perched on the edge of a small sofa. Ella Divine made herself comfortable in an enormous wingback chair with the satin of her dressing gown pooled around her. She clutched a steaming mug of tea.

"Miss Divine. About your show . . ."

Pea was clearly trying to think of a nice way to ask the singer about the troubling events. But Lou Lou couldn't contain her curiosity anymore.

"You don't always lip-synch your songs, do you? Why did you do it tonight?" The singer burst into tears. Lou

Lou felt terrible, and Pea looked at her with raised eyebrows.

"I'm so sorry!" exclaimed Lou Lou. "Please don't cry. Please. I didn't mean to make it worse. We were just surprised." And a little disappointed, thought Lou Lou, though this time she held her tongue.

"This is the first time I have ever lip-synched!" cried Ella Divine. "I promise! It was only because I came down with laryngitis yesterday and lost my singing voice." In a flash, it all made sense—the hoarseness in Ella Divine's voice, the songbird candle, and the evening's strange performance.

"How terrible!" exclaimed Pea, though she sounded relieved to know that her idol didn't normally fake her songs.

"I didn't want to cancel the show tonight and make my loyal fans wait until next month for my performance," Ella Divine explained. "The stage manager suggested that I sing along to a recording. I knew it wasn't right to fool my audience, but I was so excited to share my newest song, 'Sequined Sabine.' So I decided I would lip-synch just this one time."

"Then during 'Feathered Fedora,' the recording broke." Lou Lou filled in the next part of the story. She

thought about seeing Jeremy in the crowd. Could he have messed up the recording?

"Correct. Now I am ruined! No one will ever come to hear me sing again!" Ella Divine put her face in her hands and sobbed. Pea went to the singer and patted her shoulder.

"Miss Divine," she said, "I promise you that I, Peacock Pearl, will do everything I can to spread the truth about what happened to you tonight. I will make flyers explaining that you are not a fraud. I will tell everyone I know in the neighborhood and at school. You have my word."

"Me too," agreed Lou Lou. Ella Divine looked up. Her eyes were red but at least she was smiling.

"That would be wonderful," she said. "You are both very kind."

It was clear that Ella Divine was exhausted after her terrible evening, so Lou Lou and Pea bid her a fond farewell. Besides, they had things to do back at the SS *Lucky Alley*. There was Pinky's funeral, which was planned for tomorrow, more preparation for Día de los Muertos, and now they had flyers to make for Ella Divine. Also, there was no forgetting that they had a growing Mural Mystery to solve. It was going to be a busy weekend.

CHAPTER SEVENTEEN
Poor Elmira

Back in the crow's nest, Lou Lou and Pea made Ella Divine's flyers while they watched out Lou Lou's window for any shenanigans in the garden below.

"Something is down there!" said Pea, careful not to topple a bottle of glue as she grabbed the binoculars.

"Really? Is it Jeremy?" Lou Lou looked up from sprinkling gold glitter on construction paper.

"No, too small. And furry. Maybe a raccoon? It's eating the garbage." Pea grimaced. "Disgusting. Definitely a raccoon."

Aside from the raccoon, nothing interesting happened

outside. But Lou Lou and Pea successfully made fifty-nine flyers for Ella Divine before they went to bed. They drew pictures of the singer, the Heliotrope, Francesca, and even chocolate cheesecake. The flyers were all slightly different. But each one had the same message— explaining the lip-synching incident and asking Ella Divine's loyal fans to forgive her and return for the next show.

After eating their fill of banana pancakes in the morning, Lou Lou and Pea went to spread the truth about Ella Divine to the neighborhood. They posted their flyers on the bulletin board at the library, left a stack at Green Thumb, dropped some off at Cupcake Cabana, and gave them to passersby they recognized as fans. By eleven-thirty they were tired, hungry, and nearly out of flyers.

"Mission almost accomplished!" said Pea. "If we leave the rest of the flyers at the candle shop, we will be done."

Elmira was unlocking the front door when Lou Lou and Pea arrived.

"¡Hola, Elmira!" called Lou Lou. "You're opening late this morning."

"Yes, yes, Lou Lou Bombay. But a late morning is merely an early afternoon." Lou Lou decided she'd remember Elmira's wisdom in case she was ever late for school.

As they followed Elmira inside the candle shop, she said, "Niñas, I thought you might visit me today. What can I do for you?"

Pea held out the last of their flyers and a bit of glitter sprinkled to the floor. "We are trying to tell everyone that Ella Divine is not a fraud."

Elmira squinted at the flyer. "Ah yes," the Candle Lady said. "I heard about her miserable musical misfortune. It's kind of you to make these. What friendly 'Feathered Fedora' fans you are!"

"Can we leave them with you?" Lou Lou asked. "Maybe you could put one in the window."

"Of course!" Elmira replied. She looked up from the flyer and smiled. "Ella Divine is a wonderful singer. And ella es muy bonita and very nice. She is actually a customer of mine. I imagine she will be in later for a Perdón candle to ensure her fans' forgiveness."

"Muchas gracias," said Pea. "We really appreciate it."

"De nada," Elmira replied. "Lou Lou, do you have any more news about the changing murals? I have been thinking about them as promised, but I have yet to reach any conclusions."

"We haven't figured out what they mean but we're still working on the Mural Mystery," said Lou Lou.

Elmira nodded. "If my intuition tells me anything, you will be the first to know. But one should not get lost in the details and forget what truly matters," the Candle Lady advised. "So I hope you will not worry too much. Especially since I know you have a marvelous crop of toad lilies to think about!"

"Thanks to the Crecer candle!" Lou Lou replied. Her

stomach growled, telling her that it was time to return to the SS *Lucky Alley* for sandwiches and her dad's sour sailor lemonade. "We should probably go now."

"One more thing," said the Candle Lady. "Will you be attending the Día de los Muertos procession, niñas?"

"Absolutely," replied Lou Lou. "We never miss it."

"Then may I recommend you burn a Buena Suerte candle for good luck, just to ensure that your outfit and altar making go well. Nothing ruins a procession like poor preparation, my dears," advised Elmira.

"Thank you. Maybe another day." While Lou Lou would have liked a candle to guarantee their success, she knew it was not practical. The last time she'd burned the Crecer candle, it triggered the crow's nest smoke alarm, causing a fire scare aboard the SS *Lucky Alley*. Lou Lou was now strictly forbidden from indoor candle burning for the foreseeable future.

"Of course," said Elmira. "I may have a different good luck charm for your preparations. Wait, please." The Candle Lady disappeared behind the curtain into the shop's back room. She had been gone for only a second when Lou Lou and Pea heard a shriek. They rushed to the curtain and pushed it aside.

The back room looked like it had been hit by a tornado. A shelf was toppled and a jumble of burgundy

Éxito candles for success, dark green Sabiduría candles for wisdom, and black Protección candles were strewn across the floor. A chair was upside down, the drawers of a small mahogany desk hung open, and the papers inside were in disarray. But Elmira was not looking at the mess. Instead she was staring at a small silver box on the desk. It was open, revealing a plush red interior.

"It's gone!" the Candle Lady cried, looking from the empty box to Lou Lou and Pea and back again.

"What's gone, Elmira?" asked Lou Lou.

"My money! I only keep a small sum in the cash register up front. The rest is in this box. Or *was* in this box." Elmira finally surveyed the destruction in the room. "¡Qué desastre! I have been . . . robbed!" Elmira put her face in her hands.

"How awful! When could this have happened, Elmira?" Pea asked.

"Probably overnight. The thief must have come in and out from there." Elmira waved her hand at the open back door. "Sometimes I forget to lock the back when I close the shop. So very foolish of me." Elmira shook her head sadly. "Three weeks of profits. Stolen! What will I do now? How will I pay for my Candle Lady Caribbean Cruise?" A sob escaped her.

"Your what?" asked Lou Lou. Elmira pointed to a poster on the wall. It was a glossy picture of a large cruise ship anchored between two palm-fringed islands. The ship's rails were decorated with candles exactly like the ones in Elmira's shop. Smiling women in sunglasses held brightly colored drinks with umbrellas in them and waved from the deck. Below the picture was written:

Calling all candle ladies! Come join your candle-loving companions on the Fifth Annual Candle Lady Caribbean Cruise! Make friends, enjoy paradise, and relax by the flickering flames. You may even win the candle lady beauty contest. Hurry to register by November 15, before tickets sell out!

"This was going to be my first getaway in years," Elmira said sadly. "I was so looking forward to chatting with other candle ladies, playing Guess That Flame, and meeting Lydia Luz, the world's leading . . . candle-ologist!" The last part came out in another sob.

"I am so sorry, Elmira," said Pea, crossing the room to give the Candle Lady a hug.

"Do you know who could have done this?" Lou Lou asked, thinking of a spiky-blue-haired boy with a studded bracelet.

"No tengo idea," Elmira said.

"Maybe you should call the police," Pea suggested.

"Of course. Once I get this mess cleaned up," said the Candle Lady.

"We'll help you!" Lou Lou and Pea hefted the shelves upright and picked up candles that had rolled across the floor.

"It's good that none of these were damaged when they fell," said Lou Lou, turning over a glass pillar in her hand. She tapped her red-sneakered foot against the concrete. "The floor is pretty hard."

Pea shrugged. "Yes, but the glass is thick. It is lucky for Elmira. It would be terrible if she'd lost both her money and her candles."

When they'd finally collected the last runaway candle and returned it to the shelf, it was well past lunchtime and Lou Lou was eager to get home. Before they left, Lou Lou picked up the Buena Suerte candle recommended by Elmira for their Día de los Muertos preparations.

"I'd like to buy this candle after all," she called to Elmira, who was still in the back room.

"But you are not allowed to burn it," Pea whispered.

"My parents only said no *indoor* burning, so technically I could light it *outside* the house." Pea looked skeptical. "Plus, it's the least I can do for Elmira after the robbery." At that, Pea smiled her approval.

It was only after they'd left that Lou Lou remembered the other good luck charm that Elmira had gone to fetch in the back room. Elmira seemed to have forgotten about it, but the Candle Lady had a lot on her mind.

They'd almost made it back to the SS *Lucky Alley* without any further surprises when Pea noticed the mural on the side of Ruby's Beauty Parlor.

"Lou Lou, look!" Pea pointed at *If Pigs Could Fly*, a painting of a cloud-filled sky and bright pink pigs with angel wings and halos. "Ella Divine is in the mural!"

Lou Lou felt a distinct sense of déjà vu. Once again, a familiar scene had changed. An elegant woman now stood on one of the clouds where she hadn't been before. The scarlet-lipped figure wore a long emerald evening gown and held a microphone in one hand and a broken record in the other. Lou Lou could tell from Pea's down-turned mouth and wide blue eyes that she was upset by the reminder of her idol's bad night.

"Ella Divine will be okay." Lou Lou touched Pea's arm. "And we'll figure out what happened with the recording. Someone must have broken it if Ella Divine is in a mural!"

Helado the missing bunny, Magdalena's ruined dress, Pinky's planticide, Danielle Desserts's necklace—it was clear that the new mural images all showed some-one's cruel mischief, not accidents.

"I think you are right," Pea agreed. "But the crimes are piling up fast. How are we going to stop them?" She sounded worried.

"Listen, I know we can solve this Mural Mystery, Pea. Remember how we figured out that Mrs. Jackson's dog was stealing churros from the taco truck? Or when we helped your babysitter uncover who was sending her love letters?"

Pea bit her lip and nodded. "We are quite good at solving problems," she said. Pea raised her chin and pulled her shoulders back. "And we definitely have to get to the bottom of *this* one. For the sake of Ella Divine, Pinky, and everyone else who was hurt by these crimes, including Elmira!"

"Yes, poor Elmira," replied Lou Lou. "I bet she'll be painted next."

CHAPTER EIGHTEEN
A Funeral for Dear Pinky

Even though they were tired after the eventful morning, Lou Lou wanted to do some gardening before Pinky's funeral. While Lou Lou dug in the soil of Bouquet Blooms, Pea peeked over the fence into the neighbor's yard.

"What do you see?" Lou Lou called as she patted dirt over rows of tulip and daffodil bulbs.

"Jeremy is not there, but his jacket is on the lawn chair."

"Anything suspicious about it? Drips of mural paint on the sleeves? Bleach spots?" Lou Lou asked.

"Nothing like that. But I do see something poking

out of the pocket. A slip of paper with letters and numbers." Lou Lou brushed soil off her hands and joined Pea at the fence.

Pea squinted. "I can't make out what it says. Wait, I have an idea." Pea ran inside and came back with the binoculars.

"Okay, the numbers are 8998. And the letters are *O-S-A*."

"O-S-A. What does that mean?" Lou Lou wondered.

"I don't know. But it looks like there is another letter, half-hidden. Maybe a *B* or an *R* . . ."

"*Rosa!*" Lou Lou exclaimed. She grabbed Pea's arm, and Pea looked sideways at Lou Lou's hand.

"Sorry." Lou Lou tried to brush her dirty fingerprints off Pea's skin. Pea took her handkerchief from her pocket, wiped off the smudges, and peered through the binoculars again.

"I think there is a dash before the numbers," Pea said. "So it's probably Rosa's phone number. Why would Jeremy have her number?"

"Like I told you, he's definitely trying to get her to pay a ransom for Helado!" cried Lou Lou. "Let's call her and ask about it!"

"But how will we find the missing numbers?" Pea asked.

"We'll try some common three-digit extensions." Lou Lou was already running inside for the phone. When she returned, they tried the first combination of numbers.

"Getty's Pizza Parlor. May I take your order?" a man said on the other line.

"Uh, sorry, wrong number," Lou Lou mumbled. She dialed another combination.

"Bueno?" It was a woman, but she sounded older than Rosa. Lou Lou handed the phone to Pea.

"Buenos días. ¿Me puede comunicar con Rosa?" Pea asked politely.

"Número equivocado," the woman replied.

"Gracias. Adiós." Pea shook her head at Lou Lou. They tried five more times with no luck.

"We are not getting anywhere," Pea said. Lou Lou nodded. They couldn't call every possible combination.

"We'll just look up her number!" Lou Lou suggested. "What's her last name?"

"I don't know," replied Pea.

Lou Lou thought back to Helado's mournful painted eyes and Rosa's despair over the bunnynapping of her pet. She wished they could find Helado for Rosa.

"Maybe Jeremy is hiding Helado in the house. We could try to get in there to look!"

"Is that really a good idea?" Pea asked. "What if he catches us? Or if his parents are home?"

"Yeah, you're right," replied Lou Lou. "We need another plan. Let's go inside and think about it."

Lou Lou and Pea lounged in the living room. Soothing sounds of the sea came from speakers on the mantel, half-hidden by Halloween cobwebs. Lou Lou brought a plate of cookies from the kitchen.

"These are delicious. Did your dad make them?" Pea asked.

"Nope, he doesn't do chocolate chip because he couldn't think of a clever enough nautical name. They must've come from the store." Lou Lou and Pea munched silently until Lou Lou spoke over the high-pitched cry of a seagull.

"I don't know how to find Helado, but I have a different plan. We should make a chart of the new paintings and the bad things that have happened in the Mural Mystery. We'll call it the Mural Mystery Matrix! Maybe it will help us to see connections and figure out what's going on."

"Great idea, but we still need to make the altar and our procession outfits, too," said Pea. "Día de los Muertos is this Wednesday and we have barely started!"

"And there's also Pinky's funeral," Lou Lou said.

"We should do that first," replied Pea. "It's important for you, Lou Lou. And for Pinky."

"Of course." Pea was right—it was time to finally say goodbye to her camellia. "Matrix making will be tonight's activity and we'll work on the altar and our procession outfits tomorrow. Let us now step outside for the funeral," Lou Lou said formally. "Mom, Dad! You are cordially invited to join us for a small service to bid farewell to the best camellia ever to grace the garden of the SS *Lucky Alley*."

Lou Lou fetched a shopping bag from the crow's nest and followed Pea out to the garden to stand near Pinky's resting place. Lou Lou's dad looked solemn in his captain's hat and her mom held a bouquet of magenta origami flowers.

"This will be a simple service since the real memorial will be on Día de los Muertos," Lou Lou began. "But I have brought some items and prepared a few words." She reached into the shopping bag and pulled out an old pickle jar full of water, which she held high in the air.

"This sacred water is from the tap at Green Thumb nursery to remind Pinky's spirit of its camellia childhood." Lou Lou placed the jar at her feet and took from the bag a homemade blue ribbon.

"We all know that Pinky would have won first place in the Flowering Bushes and Shrubs competition at the Hello Horticulture! Society Annual Conference. This is the honor that Pinky deserves!" Lou Lou placed the ribbon near the avocado tree and pulled out a photo of herself and Pinky taken the first year that Pinky flowered. Lou Lou was smiling and holding one of Pinky's blooms close to the camera to show the bright color of the petals.

"Although I may grow other camellias, I will always remember Pinky as my best friend."

Pea cleared her throat.

"Best *plant* friend, I mean." Lou Lou put the photo next to the ribbon. The last item in the bag was the Crecer candle. "Pinky will grow no more, at least in this world, but this symbolizes Pinky's life."

"Lou Lou . . ." Pea said hesitantly, eyeing Lou Lou's parents.

"We're *outside* the house," Lou Lou reminded Pea.

"It's okay. Just blow it out when you're done," said her mom. Lou Lou handed Pea the candle to hold as she struck a match.

"It is now time for the eulogy."

Lou Lou pulled a small piece of paper from her pocket and everyone bowed their heads as she began to read:

Ode to Pinky

You started so small, no blooms at all,
But then grew so tall.
And in the fall
With beautiful blossoms, you did enthrall.
You were more than a shrub,
You were more than a plant—
A beautiful thing that did ever enchant.
You brightened the garden
Of the SS Lucky Alley,
A masterpiece till your tragic finale,
And you would have won
A ribbon so blue.
No other camellia
Could compare to you.
But you've moved on to a place
Full of water and light,
A heavenly space
Free of aphids and blight.
Although it's the end
And you've gone away,
You're still loved by your friend
Lou Lou Bombay.

When she'd finished, Lou Lou picked up the jar of water. She'd planned to only sprinkle a little on the ground but decided to pour out the whole jar, careful to avoid the photograph and the ribbon. After all, camellias like water, Lou Lou thought. Any good

horticulturist knew that a too-dry camellia would bear undersize flowers and even risk bud-drop.

Lou Lou's mom placed the origami bouquet by the photo and her dad held out a small bundle. "I wrapped one of Pinky's branches in sailcloth," he explained, putting the bundle with the other items. "It's what we'd do if we were having a burial at sea."

"Rest in peace, Pinky," Pea said, and with those words, the funeral for dear Pinky was over.

Now it was time to catch the camellia's killer!

CHAPTER NINETEEN
The Mural Mystery Matrix

After Pinky's funeral, Lou Lou was eager to start on the Mural Mystery Matrix. But the call for dinner came before they made any progress.

Lou Lou's dad rang the large old-fashioned bell and yelled, "Chow time! All hands to the galley!"

It was pirate pizza night, so Lou Lou didn't really mind the interruption. Pirate pizza was a delicious combination of cheese, tomato sauce, basil or oregano from Eats and Cures, and a single pepperoni eye patch on each slice. Once she and Pea had cleaned their plates, Lou Lou asked to be excused.

Her dad frowned and said, "Lou Lou, can't you wait for my limey key lime pie? Keeps the scurvy away." Pea politely muffled a laugh with her napkin.

"But we have important things to do."

"May we take it to go?" Pea tried to help. Lou Lou kicked her gently under the table. "I mean, may we eat it in our berths, Captain?"

"I suppose that's fine. I don't want to get in the way of 'important things.'" Lou Lou's dad served up generous slices of pie.

They were ready to head up to the crow's nest, plates in hand, when Lou Lou's mom asked, "That new neighbor boy—what's his name? Joseph? Joshua?"

"Jeremy." Lou Lou tried not to hiss.

"Jeremy, right. He came by today with his parents."

"He what?" squeaked Lou Lou, nearly dropping her plate.

"He came by," Lou Lou's mom repeated, clearly not realizing the significance of this. "You girls were out with your Ella Divine flyers. He seems charming. I told him he could come back later, but his parents said they would be busy for the rest of the day."

"What did he want?" asked Lou Lou, her voice still shrill.

"He was just being neighborly. He wanted to say hello to you, and Mr. and Mrs. Ruiz wanted to meet us. Jeremy even gave me a plate of chocolate chip cookies," her mom answered. "Oh, and I almost forgot—he brought you something else." Lou Lou's mom disappeared into the kitchen. She returned a moment later and handed Lou Lou a book with a glossy cover that read *Caring for Your Camellia: A Comprehensive Guide to Nurturing Award-Winning Blooms*. "I thought it was very nice of him. I didn't have the heart to tell him about Pinky's passing."

Lou Lou's ears were bright red. Not only was Jeremy the prime suspect in Pinky's planticide, but he seemed to be mocking Lou Lou by giving her a camellia book when he *knew* that Pinky was dead. And he had some nerve bringing over yummy chocolate chip cookies to keep up his nice-guy charade. What if he'd poisoned the cookies just like he'd poisoned Pinky?

Lou Lou did a mental check of her body: Stomach, okay. Pulse, okay. Ears, hot, but that was nothing new. Still, Lou Lou wanted to put down her pie and march over to her neighbor's house right that moment to confront Jeremy.

Pea touched Lou Lou on the arm, sensing that she

was about to do something impulsive and probably unwise.

"How about that chart?" Pea asked.

Chrysanthemum, chrysanthemum, chrysanthemum, Lou Lou thought, and she calmed down. Yes, they should stick to the plan.

"What chart?" asked Lou Lou's mom.

"Just another one of our projects," said Lou Lou.

"Thank you for the limey key lime pie, Peter," Pea called as they hurried up the rope ladder.

In the crow's nest, Lou Lou held the camellia book by the spine and shook it vigorously over the floor.

"What are you doing?" Pea asked.

"Looking for evidence or threats from Jeremy." Lou Lou thumbed through the pages but all she saw were colored pictures of camellia varieties. Finally, she gave up and shoved the book into a space on her shelf.

"Some nerve he has, giving me a camellia book. Because of him, I don't even have a camellia!" Lou Lou went to the window and looked at her garden. The asters were now thriving alongside the toad lilies. Lou Lou took a deep breath. There was nothing she could do but move forward to solve the Mural Mystery. "Let's start the Matrix."

Lou Lou and Pea's Matrix-making went quickly. Pea drew perfect lines and boxes with a ruler, and Lou Lou added words, names, and X's.

"Remember when we made charts in first grade?" Lou Lou asked.

"Of course! Mine showed my cleaning chores and yours showed the days that you watered your cactus," replied Pea.

"And Kyle spilled his chocolate milk on your chart," Lou Lou said, drawing another X.

Pea scowled, then smiled. "You helped me make a new one, though, and we've been best friends ever since!"

As they talked, the Matrix became a marker-drawn masterpiece that clearly showed which murals memorialized which crimes, and the human/animal/camellia victims to match. Lou Lou didn't expect that the Matrix would miraculously solve the Mural Mystery, but she hoped it might bring them closer to a solution.

Lou Lou added the final X in the *Ella Divine's Musical Misfortune* row under *If Pigs Could Fly*. She leaned back and squinted at the Mural Mystery Matrix:

MURAL MYSTERY MATRIX

EVENT/VICTIM	MURAL				
	LADY CARMEN RIDES BONITO	SCHOOL IS FOR THE BIRDS	A LOVELY DAY FOR A PARADE	DANCING IN SPACE	IF PIGS COULD FLY
HELADO THE WHITE BUNNY	X				
MAGDALENA'S QUINCEAÑERA DRESS DISASTER		X			
DEAR PINKY'S INCREDIBLY TRAGIC PLANTICIDE			X		
DANIELLE DESSERTS'S STARRY NECKLACE				X	
ELLA DIVINE'S MUSICAL MISFORTUNE					X

IF FOUND PLEASE RETURN TO LOU LOU BOMBAY OR PEACOCK PEARL

"I don't see any connections between the events and the original mural paintings. I mean, Pinky is in *A Lovely Day for a Parade*. But what does a camellia have to do with parades?"

"And how could Ella Divine's broken recording possibly be related to flying pigs?" Pea asked.

"Well, at least we have all the Mural Mystery information in one place now. That's helpful. Maybe we should also make a list of the suspects' known whereabouts. Speaking of which . . ." Something caught Lou Lou's eye and she peered out her little window, pressing her nose against the glass.

"Pea, come look! He's in my yard!"

"¿De verdad? What is he doing?" Pea rushed to the window. On the grass below was a figure dressed in black. They couldn't see all his features, but the loping walk and spiky hair told them it was definitely Jeremy.

"I'm not sure," Lou Lou replied. "But he better not touch a petal or leaf on any of my plants!"

Jeremy went straight to Pinky's former spot under the avocado tree. Lou Lou had brought all the funeral mementos into the house, so it was just an empty patch of wet dirt. He took a small paper bag from the sack slung over his shoulder and peeked inside, then reached in and pulled something out. Jeremy stooped toward the ground with his back to the window.

"What was in that bag?" cried Lou Lou, thinking her ears might actually become little fireballs. "Did it look like bleach? Or vinegar? Or a hammer? If he even sets a foot near my perennial sunflowers, he's gonna be sorry!"

"It's too dark and I can't see well from this angle," Pea replied, looking through the binoculars. "But he's not pouring anything and I don't see any hammers."

Jeremy stood up and crumpled the paper bag in his fist, stuffing it into his sack. He walked back toward the fence.

"I'm going to find out what's going on!" Lou Lou pulled on her sweatshirt and hat. Pea shook her head.

"Lou Lou, you cannot go out there right now."

"Why not? We caught him in the act, Pea! Okay, I'm not sure what act, but I know it was a bad one. Even if he doesn't harm anything else in the garden, we still have to confront him to get justice for Pinky . . . and for Magdalena and Ella Divine!" Lou Lou remembered to add the people Pea cared about most. She began to climb down the rope ladder.

"Lou Lou, if we let Jeremy know we are on to him, we might never be able to prove that he is behind the crimes. Not to mention, Rosa might not get Helado back, Elmira might never see her money again, and Danielle's necklace might be lost forever. We are still better off watching him secretly for a while. He is not going to confess, so it will be his word against ours until we have more evidence."

Lou Lou paused to run through her second set of *chrysanthemum*s that evening. Although she wanted to avenge Pinky's death immediately, Pea made a good point, as usual.

"I suppose you're right," Lou Lou replied. "But he knew exactly where Pinky *was*, so that's some proof he committed the planticide, right? Is he still there?"

"No, he's gone now," said Pea. "It's too dark out there to see anything anyway."

Lou Lou climbed back up the ladder and pulled off her hat. Her head itched from the wool. "First thing tomorrow, we'll go outside and try to figure out what Jeremy was doing down there, okay?" she said.

"Yes, perfect pla . . . ahhh . . . n." Pea covered her mouth as she yawned. It was late and they'd had a long day.

Although Lou Lou wanted to stay awake to see if Jeremy returned, before they knew it, they were both fast asleep.

CHAPTER TWENTY
An Altar Is Born

It rained during the night, but Sunday brought sunshine, and Lou Lou awoke with a sense of purpose. She was *almost* certain she knew who had killed Pinky and she suspected Jeremy was also behind the other crimes. Now she and Pea had to prove he was responsible and stop him from causing more mayhem.

Lou Lou sat up in bed and pushed curls out of her eyes. Pea was still sleeping.

"Pea!" Lou Lou whispered, but there was no response. She patted Pea's arm.

"Demasiado temprano," Pea groaned and rolled away from Lou Lou. "Too early!"

"It's after eight. We have a lot to do today," Lou Lou pressed.

Pea half opened her eyes, then closed them again. "Muffin and tea, please," she requested.

"Coming right up!" Lou Lou knew she'd won the rise-and-shine battle. She hurried down to the kitchen and returned a few minutes later. Using the pulley and bucket that brought things to and from the crow's nest, Lou Lou hauled up a steaming cup of tea and a plate of cinnamon muffins. The tea sloshed onto the muffins during its journey in the bucket, but Pea didn't seem to mind. She sat up in bed in her striped pajamas and took a sip from the mug.

"First we'll go outside and see if we can figure out what Jeremy was doing last night," Lou Lou said. Pea pulled a brush through her hair while Lou Lou riffled through Pea's duffel bag for a T-shirt and jeans to move her along. Pea raised an eyebrow.

"Don't worry, I will fold everything back up," said Lou Lou.

"The shirt with the bluebirds goes well with them." Pea pointed at the jeans and Lou Lou handed her the clothes.

"We'll work on our Día de los Muertos preparations after we look for Jeremy evidence."

Pea's mouth was full of soggy muffin, so she nodded in reply.

In the backyard, Lou Lou and Pea examined the area around the avocado tree. Pea wore gloves and stayed a safe distance from the dirt, while Lou Lou crawled in the soil on hands and knees, looking for signs of Jeremy's mischief. She also carefully checked Bouquet Blooms, Summer Weirds, Eats and Cures, and Fancy Fall Florals. But she found no foul play—in fact, her perennial sunflowers were doing better than ever. And, aside from a bit of displaced dirt and a few faint boot prints, there was also no trace of Jeremy's activity near the avocado tree. Everything looked the same, just a bit wetter from the nighttime rain.

"It's frustrating. If only we could find something . . . *anything* that would link him directly to the crimes," Lou Lou said.

"We will just have to keep looking," Pea replied. Lou Lou agreed—they had to wait for Jeremy to make a mistake. But first they had procession outfits to create and an altar to make.

Back inside, Lou Lou and Pea fetched paper, fabric, thread, glue, and other odds and ends. They laid everything on the living room floor next to the unlit Buena Suerte candle that Lou Lou hoped would help with their preparations. After three hours of hard work on their outfits and Pinky's altar, they were done. Pea added blue lace to her embroidered skirt and small pearl buttons to her sweater. But Pea's pièce de résistance was her parasol. She attached a rainbow of tassels to the outer edge of an old umbrella. They swirled wildly as she twirled around the room.

Lou Lou had a long black dress, a hand-me-down from her mom made smaller. Keeping with her Pinky theme, she cut out colorful velvet flowers, and Pea helped her sew them to the dress and finish them off with button centers. She couldn't hold a parasol in the procession because she had to carry Pinky's altar. But she'd found a large-brimmed hat and pinned on multicolored tassels for a similar effect. Lou Lou realized the slight flaw in her design when she triumphantly put on the hat but had to brush orange and green strings aside in order to see. With a bit of trimming, though, the hat was perfect.

Lou Lou's mom came into the living room, sneezing

but smiling. She gave Lou Lou three origami flowers, more elaborate than the simple bouquet she'd created for Pinky's funeral.

"*Achoo!* Fantastic!" she exclaimed, talking about the altar, not her sneeze.

"¡Salud!" said Pea.

"Are you okay?" Lou Lou asked. Her mom's eyes were watery and her nose was red.

"First cold of the season," her mom said in a nasally voice. "I need a tiss—*Achoo!*" She hurried toward the bathroom.

"Bless you—I mean, salud!" Lou Lou attached the flowers to the altar by wrapping the wire stems around the wooden frame. Inside the frame, Lou Lou had fastened mementos and symbols of Pinky. She replaced the photo of Bisabuela Nellie and her terriers with the photograph she had used at the funeral. She also added construction-paper sunshine, water, and soil, as well as an advertisement for Pinky's favorite brand of fertilizer cut from the Hello Horticulture! Society magazine. The final touch was a spritz of Lou Lou's mom's floral perfume, even though it smelled like jasmine and not autumn queen camellia.

"Looks wonderful," Pea said. "Pinky would be honored." With the Día de los Muertos projects complete, Lou Lou and Pea took everything up to the crow's nest for safekeeping until Wednesday evening.

"What now?" asked Pea.

"The Mural Mystery, of course," replied Lou Lou. "But first, let's eat. I know better than to sleuth on an empty stomach!"

CHAPTER TWENTY-ONE
A Storm for Sugar Skulls Sarah

During lunch, Lou Lou and Pea talked about the procession.

"Magdalena will come with us," Pea said.

"That's terrific!" replied Lou Lou. Because Pea's cousin had agreed to accompany them, Lou Lou and Pea could walk in the evening procession without their parents' constant supervision.

Lou Lou's mom coughed loudly as she joined them at the table. Lou Lou wheeled the fridge open and took out a carton of orange juice. She poured a glass for her mom.

"Thanks, honey." Jane took a big sip. "Could you girls do me a favor? I need some cold medicine and your dad had to go to—"

"Sure!" Lou Lou answered before her mom could finish. Although she was happy to help, a trip to the pharmacy would also give them a chance to see any new changes to the murals. It didn't hurt that Cupcake Cabana was on the way. Lou Lou's mom knew this, too, and gave Lou Lou money for medicine plus a little more.

"For cherry cough syrup and sweets for my sweets." Jane patted Lou Lou on the head and winked at Pea. "Back to bed now for me. What a shame to miss such a lovely day."

Lou Lou kept an eye on the murals as they ate their cupcakes and walked toward the pharmacy. She'd brought along the Mural Mystery Matrix and a pen, and she checked the Matrix every time they passed an important mural to make sure they'd recorded all the additions correctly. Everything seemed in order and there were no new changes.

"Maybe it will be a quiet day for the Mural Mystery," Pea suggested.

Before Lou Lou could reply, a scream pierced the midday calm. Lou Lou sprinted in the direction of another scream, with Pea close behind. When they rounded the corner, they saw that it was Sugar Skulls Sarah making the racket. She stood in front of her studio, dripping wet. A puddle formed around her on the sidewalk.

"What happened, Sarah?" panted Lou Lou.

Sarah took off her glasses and pushed sopping strands of hair off her face. Drips ran down her cheeks. She might have been crying, but with all the water Lou Lou couldn't tell.

"It's just awful. Really truly awful," Sarah wailed. "Everything is soaked."

"Yes, we can see that," replied Lou Lou impatiently. Pea shot her a *try to be more sensitive* glance. Gently, Lou Lou continued. "Maybe we can help. Should I go find you a towel?"

Sugar Skulls Sarah wrung out the cuffs of her sweater, making another puddle at Lou Lou's feet. "It's not just me that's wet, Lou Lou. Like I said, *everything* is soaked." Sarah pointed at her studio.

Through the open glass door Lou Lou and Pea saw what she meant. Inside, it looked like there had been a torrential downpour. Water ran down the legs of tables and chairs. Many of the wall tapestries were drenched and askew. The marigold vases were overflowing, and decorations spilled out of bowls in the flood, speckling the floor with glitter and bright color.

"What in the world—?" Pea started to ask.

"The sprinklers!" cried Sarah. "I was putting the finishing touches on some of the skulls when the fire sprinklers in the studio turned on at full blast. But there was no fire! Not even a puff of smoke." Lou Lou and Pea suddenly realized the full consequences of the sprinkler storm.

"The sugar skulls!" exclaimed Pea. "They will dissolve!"

"Exactly," Sarah responded sadly. "They're ruined." She pointed at shelves that had once displayed the skulls she'd decorated for the giant wagon she always towed behind her bicycle in the procession. Sure enough, the skulls were now formless lumps of white covered in wet feathers and dripping clusters of beads and gems. It was a mess.

"How terrible!" Pea cried, clearly distressed by the thought of destroyed artwork. "What can we do?"

"It's hopeless," replied Sarah. "I'll have to start over and work night and day just to make enough skulls for Día de los Muertos. ¡Ay, qué pena!" Lou Lou heard sirens in the distance. Sarah sighed.

"Before I do anything, I have to explain this to the fire department and clean up this disaster."

"We'd stay to help you clean . . ." Lou Lou said.

"Yes, normally we would love to!" Pea chimed in.

". . . but we're supposed to go to the pharmacy." Lou Lou remembered the medicine they'd promised her mom.

"No hay problema," said Sarah. "I'm going to call some friends to come over."

Sugar Skulls Sarah went back into her studio. Lou Lou and Pea stood gazing after her for a silent moment.

Then Lou Lou said, "Sprinkler sabotage! It's gotta be! You heard her—there wasn't a fire. There's no way this was an accident."

"Someone could have turned on the sprinklers when Sarah's back was turned," Pea said.

"Jeremy! He was in the studio when we made our sugar skulls," Lou Lou remembered. "He probably scoped it out so he could ruin everything later!"

Pea pointed down the block. "Look, here comes Elmira!" The Candle Lady hurried toward them. The brown fabric of her shapeless clothing billowed out around her.

"Hi, Elmira!" Lou Lou called.

"¡Hola, Lou Lou Bombay y Peacock Pearl! How are

you today, my dears? Have you made any progress on the—"

"Mural Mystery!" Lou Lou finished Elmira's sentence. "Don't worry—we're definitely getting closer to proving who is behind the crimes. We have to stop tragedies like this." Lou Lou pointed at Sarah's Studio. Inside, Sarah was mopping the floor.

"You're right. ¡Estoy totalmente de acuerdo!" said Elmira, looking vexed. "I was so sad for Sarah when she called to tell me about her soggy sprinkler storm surprise. I rushed here to bring her this candle." Elmira held up a candle that said *Reparar*, and had a picture of a man with a hammer and a nail. "I do not have a 'dry' candle so I chose the next best one, a 'repair' candle," she explained.

"Did you find any clues about who robbed you, Elmira?" Lou Lou asked.

"Regrettably, no." The Candle Lady sounded sad.

"I'm sorry to hear that," Lou Lou said. "I think my new neighbor, Jeremy, committed the other crimes. He probably stole your money, too! Do you know him?"

"I have met him," the Candle Lady replied. "He seemed like un buen niño, but who knows? Las cosas no siempre son lo que parecen."

"Things are not always what they seem," Pea translated. "I hope you can still go on your vacation," she said to Elmira.

"Gracias, niña. You are very kind, pero no es posible." Elmira changed the subject. "I should head into the studio now."

"Adiós," Pea said to the Candle Lady. The girls watched as one of their favorite neighbors rushed to help another.

CHAPTER TWENTY-TWO
Hallow-What?

After Pea went home, Lou Lou spent the rest of Sunday afternoon weeding her garden and finishing homework. She couldn't help peeking at *Caring for Your Camellia* and admiring the different varieties. When she'd looked at the apple blossom camellias and turned next to the autumn queen page, a wave of sadness for poor Pinky washed over her.

Monday was the first day of the three-day celebration of Día de los Muertos, so before bed on Sunday, Lou Lou cleared her desk and set up a tribute to Pinky. The centerpiece was the altar, next to which Lou Lou placed her sugar skull and a vase of marigolds from Green

Thumb. She also laid out traditional pan de muerto, bread of the dead, made by Pea and her abuela. Pan de muerto was a sweet bread often topped with bone shapes. But Pea had decorated Pinky's pan de muerto with flower shapes and magenta sugar sprinkles instead. The orange flower water in the recipe made it extra special for Pinky.

When she woke up on Monday morning, Lou Lou spent a few minutes looking at the tribute and thinking of the good times with Pinky.

"I remember your first flower," she said aloud to the spirit of her camellia. "I knew right away that I'd grown a blue-ribbon contender!"

"Lou Lou?" her mom called from below, interrupting Lou Lou's reminiscing.

"I'm almost ready for school!"

"Okay. But I was wondering if you want your ladybug wings for your Halloween costume."

"Hallow-what? Oh, right!" Lou Lou smacked her forehead. With all that had happened the past few days, she'd forgotten today was Halloween. Her whole school would be a mass of wizards, goblins, and princesses.

Each year, Lou Lou alternated costumes between the scariest horticulture insect threat, the aphid, and the insect that was dearest to her heart, the ladybug. While most people liked ladybugs for their pretty markings, Lou Lou liked them because they ate dreaded aphids for dinner. This was a ladybug year.

Lou Lou quickly pulled on a red dress with black spots.

"Do you have my antennae, Mom?"

"I can't find them, honey." Lou Lou did a quick sweep of the crow's nest for the antennae but they were nowhere to be seen. She grabbed a black headband and some pipe cleaners from her art supplies box and quickly made a makeshift set before she climbed down the rope ladder.

At Lou Lou's school, the halls were packed with kids in costumes. Lou Lou's ladybug wings gently slapped the elbows of bunnies and firefighters as she made her way to English. Kyle Longfellow was dressed in a black-and-silver Comet Cop costume, complete with glossy leggings and big gloves. Lou Lou smiled when she saw that he was wearing his bumblebee sweater over his silver bodysuit, leaving his Comet Cop cape to peek out at the bottom.

In the midst of the crowd, Lou Lou heard, "Happy

Halloween, neighbor!" She froze and her ears started to burn.

"Jeremy," she growled. So far, she'd avoided him at school. The sixth-grade classrooms were on a different floor and they didn't have the same lunch period. But she'd known that she'd run into him someday. It seemed today was that day.

"Happy Halloween," she muttered. Jeremy was wearing a Dracula cape along with his usual black boots and studded bracelet. But what caught Lou Lou's eye was the black candle he held in one hand. It had a picture of a scary beast and the word *Protección* on the glass holder.

"What's that for?" she asked, pointing at the candle.

"Nothing, really," Jeremy replied. "I just thought it looked creepy and matched my costume. They won't let me light it in school, though."

"Where did you get it?" Lou Lou asked, remembering she'd seen other Protección candles strewn across the floor of the candle shop after the robbery.

"Someone gave it to me," Jeremy replied vaguely. He quickly changed the subject. "Hey, cool ladybug costume!" Jeremy grinned at Lou Lou and she saw his fake fangs. "I like that you came up with something original. Unlike *some* people."

Lou Lou followed Jeremy's gaze and saw Danielle and her snooty-girl posse gathered around Danielle's locker. They were dressed all in pink, the Sugar Mountain Sisters' favorite color. They had pink bows in their hair and wore T-shirts with pink glittery letters printed across the front. Danielle's said *Shelly*, another girl's said *Sherry*, and the other girls' shirts said *Shellytwo* and *Sherrytwo*. Clearly, there weren't enough Sugar Mountain Sisters to go around. Lou Lou noticed Danielle touch her neck and frown. Jeremy seemed to notice it, too.

"I heard that girl complaining in the gym about someone stealing her jewelry. Do you know anything about that?" Jeremy asked.

"No, do *you*?" Lou Lou tried not to sound too suspicious.

"Nada," Jeremy said. "I'm just the new guy, remember? How would I know *anything* about *anything*?"

Lou Lou narrowed her eyes.

"All right, I gotta get to Social Studies," said Jeremy. "Catch ya later. Happy Halloweeeeeen!"

Lou Lou felt unsettled as she watched Jeremy lope off down the hall. He must have stolen the Protección candle from Elmira's shop during the robbery, she thought. Had he brought up Danielle's necklace to brag about his crime, just like he'd done with Pinky's planticide? She couldn't be sure, but one thing was certain—seeing Jeremy was the creepiest thing that had happened to her so far this Halloween!

Although she had serious matters on her mind, Lou Lou's Halloween classes were fun. In art, they sketched a vampire family tree. Lou Lou's math teacher held contests to guess the weight of a pumpkin and the number of candies in a jar. Lou Lou's guess of eleven pounds, six ounces won her the pumpkin and Danielle won the candy.

"The Victoria candle is working!" Lou Lou heard Danielle tell the other Shelly and the Sherrys when she claimed her prize. "I am so totally going to win tickets to that movie premiere."

Even Miss Mash got in the Halloween spirit in Science by making a bubbling potion and cackling in her taupe witch's hat. Still, Lou Lou was excited when the day was over and she was finally sitting with Pea at the SS *Lucky Alley* kitchen table. Between them was a giant mound of candy they'd pooled after their school Halloween parties.

"Feel like going trick-or-treating?" Lou Lou bit the head off a red gummy bear.

"Yes!" Pea daintily nibbled on a marshmallow ghost. She adjusted the velvet hat she'd bought at Sparkle 'N Clean so it wouldn't fall off her head. In her beaded gown and emerald green boa, Pea made an excellent Halloween Ella Divine. "There is no such thing as too much candy. Also we can see everyone in their costumes."

"I'll go tell my mom." Lou Lou went into her parents' bedroom. Her mom, still ill, was curled up beneath a thick quilt made by Grandma Bombay and decorated with a nautical star. Lou Lou tiptoed to the bedside.

"Mom? Can Pea and I go out trick-or-treating?"

Lou Lou's mom smiled weakly.

"Sure, honey. Only as far as Twenty-Fifth Street, though. And can you bring in the mail before you leave?"

"Of course!" Lou Lou bent down and kissed her mom's forehead like her mom always did to her when Lou Lou was sick.

Before she rejoined Pea, Lou Lou went to the SS *Lucky Alley* mailbox. Among the letters and bills was an envelope with no stamp or address, just the initials *L.L.B.* printed on the outside. Lou Lou opened it as she walked into the kitchen and found a piece of ivory paper folded up inside.

"What's that?" Pea asked. There was no letterhead, greeting, or signature, just a message in black ink in the center of the page. Lou Lou read aloud:

IN ALL THE SCENES SHOWING SOMETHING NEW,
LOOK AROUND FOR THE BRIGHTEST HUE.
LEARN ITS NAME, AND ONCE YOU DO,
EACH FIRST LETTER WILL BE A CLUE.
P.S. YOU SEEK THE ONE THAT'S MISSING.

By the time she reached the word *missing,* Lou Lou's ears were as red as the gummy bears she'd been eating.

"It must be a riddle!" Lou Lou squealed. "About the Mural Mystery!"

"I think you're right!" Pea was excited, too.

"We can solve it!" Lou Lou said. She loved riddles and had never been presented with one so important. "Maybe it will point us to clues to solve the crimes. It's too bad we didn't see who put it in the mailbox."

"Even if we had, everyone is dressed up so it's diffi-cult to tell who's who. A lot of people know where you live so it could have been anyone."

"The first step is to break the riddle into pieces." For-getting about trick-or-treating, Lou Lou plunked down in a chair next to Pea and laid the paper on the table between them. Pea pulled a pen from her schoolbag.

"Okay, so the beginning is easy. **IN ALL THE SCENES SHOWING SOMETHING NEW** must mean the changed murals, right?"

"Definitely," Pea agreed. In her careful handwriting, next to the riddle's first line, Pea wrote, *SCENES SHOWING SOMETHING NEW* = *changed murals.* She looked back at Lou Lou, whose brow was furrowed in concentration.

"**LOOK AROUND FOR THE BRIGHTEST HUE** is tougher," Lou Lou said.

"*Hue* means color—" Pea began.

"All of the murals have many bright colors," said Lou Lou.

"True," Pea replied. "But the riddle says *hue*, which means just one. How will we know which one?"

"Hmm, I think we should focus on the brightest hue in the newly added images. Let's put that down as a guess." Pea agreed and next to the second line on the page she printed, *BRIGHTEST HUE* = *new color in mural addition.*

"**LEARN ITS NAME, AND ONCE YOU DO,**" Lou Lou read. "We just need to find the name of the hue."

"That sounds right," Pea said. "Good thing I brought my color swatch book." She wrote, *LEARN ITS NAME* = *name of brightest hue.*

Lou Lou read the last line of the riddle. "**EACH FIRST LETTER WILL BE A CLUE.** So we're looking for the first letter of each hue's name."

"What do we do with the first letters, once we have them all?" Pea asked.

"I don't know. We'll figure that part out later, I guess," Lou Lou said. "We can't forget the P.S. What does **YOU SEEK THE ONE THAT'S MISSING** mean?"

"I have no idea. I think we should solve the main part of the riddle first, then consider the P.S.," Pea said. "My mother is coming to pick me up at five-thirty. We don't have much time to check out the murals."

"Then let's go!" replied Lou Lou.

Seconds later, Lou Lou and Pea were out the door. Everywhere they looked, there were ghosts, ghouls, and monsters clustered in doorways holding out pillowcases and pumpkin-shaped buckets for candy.

There wasn't enough time to visit all the murals, so they went to *A Lovely Day for a Parade* and *Dancing in Space* first, since they were right next to each other. When they arrived, Lou Lou pulled the Mural Mystery

Matrix and a pen from her satchel, and Pea unfolded the creased riddle paper.

"These are **SCENES SHOWING SOMETHING NEW**, so we've got that part of the riddle covered," said Lou Lou.

"Moving on to **BRIGHTEST HUE**," Pea said.

Lou Lou looked at *Dancing in Space*. "This one's easy. Danielle's necklace is only one color so that's got to be the hue we're looking for."

"Yes, write down—" Pea stopped and began to thumb through her color swatch book.

"It's rose gold," said Lou Lou. "Danielle made sure to tell *everyone* that." In the Mural Mystery Matrix box that corresponded to *Dancing in Space* and *Danielle Desserts's Starry Necklace*, Lou Lou wrote, *Rose gold.* She thought, **EACH FIRST LETTER WILL BE A CLUE**, and underlined the *R.*

"*A Lovely Day for a Parade?*" Pea asked, nodding in the direction of the other mural.

Lou Lou took a deep breath before she turned to face Pinky in *A Lovely Day for a Parade*. She knew the best thing she could do for Pinky was to focus on solving the camellia's planticide, not cry over withered flowers. Still, she was grateful for Pea's comforting hand on her elbow as they stared at the image of the dying plant.

"There's a lot of brown." Lou Lou looked sadly at the shriveled leaves. "That could be the hue."

"Some of Pinky's painted flowers are not dried up, so there is a lot of magenta, too," said Pea, opening her swatch book to a shade that perfectly matched Pinky's healthier petals. "That is definitely the **BRIGHTEST HUE**."

In the Matrix box at the intersection of *Dear Pinky's Incredibly Tragic Planticide* and *A Lovely Day for a Parade*, Lou Lou wrote *Magenta*. She underlined the <u>*M*</u>.

"I don't get it. So far these letters don't mean anything," Lou Lou said.

"It might make sense after we add more hues," replied Pea. "But now . . ." She looked at her watch. "We have to go back. My mother is probably at your house already!"

They hurried to the SS *Lucky Alley*, hoping to beat Pea's mother. But when they arrived, Silvia Pearl was already on Lou Lou's front steps. She was holding Dos, who'd been to the vet because Uno had given him a bad swipe. Dos yowled at Lou Lou and Lou Lou yowled back. Vet or no vet, Dos was a mean cat. But he loved Pea and purred loudly when she petted him.

"Estás un poco tarde. I've been waiting for you, Pea-cock Paloma Pearl," said Silvia. *Uh-oh,* Lou Lou thought. Pea's mother only used Pea's full name when she was angry.

"It's my fault, Silvia." Lou Lou jumped to Pea's rescue. "I needed her to help me with something important because my mom is sick today." This was mostly true.

"I am sorry to hear that, Lou Lou." Silvia's tone softened. "Please tell your mom that I hope she feels better." She looked at Pea. "You need to do your homework, Miss Pea 'Ella Divine.' It's time to go." Dos yowled in agreement.

Pea handed Lou Lou the riddle. "See you tomorrow!" she said, and followed her mother to the door.

"See you tomorrow!" Lou Lou called back. "And don't forget . . ." Pea glanced over her shoulder, and Lou Lou made an M with her hands. Pea smiled in recognition and made a second M in return.

Mural Mystery.

CHAPTER TWENTY-THREE
Cats, Hats, and Bats

Tuesday was dreary and Lou Lou's sleepy eyes felt heavy. Her stomach was queasy from eating too much chocolate the night before, and the sight of gummy bears made her feel sick. Pea was wrong—there *was* such a thing as too much candy.

It was not Lou Lou's best day at school. After waking up late, she threw on mismatched clothes and skipped breakfast to prepare last minute for a discussion about famous inventors. But when she got to class, it turned out that Mr. Anthem's lesson was about geography. At lunch, Lou Lou realized that her dad had accidentally switched her turkey sandwich for his liverwurst. By the afternoon, she'd lost count of how many *chrysanthemums* she'd said to herself during the day. The only good thing was that there were no more Jeremy sightings.

When Lou Lou finally arrived back home and saw Serena smiling over the SS *Lucky Alley*'s front door, she breathed a sigh of relief. Pea was due any minute to work on the riddle and the Mural Mystery. Then the phone in the kitchen rang.

"Ahoy, you've reached the SS *Lucky Alley*. This is Lou Lou speaking."

"It's me," replied a familiar voice. "I haven't left my house yet. Uno rubbed against my paint palette and it's taking me forever to get the turquoise out of his fur."

"Drat!" said Lou Lou, who was eager to get back to riddle solving. Though she couldn't help but laugh at the thought of Pea's painted cat. "Can you ask your father to drop you off at *If Pigs Could Fly*? That way I can meet you there and we can get right to it!"

"Definitely!" said Pea. "See you in twenty minutes."

Lou Lou stuffed the Matrix and the riddle into her satchel and grabbed her coat. She put on her sneakers, then wrote her parents a note saying she had gone for a walk with Pea and would be home before dark.

On the way to *If Pigs Could Fly*, Lou Lou kept an eye on the other murals and, sure enough, the Mural Mystery had struck again. On the side of a garage was a mural that Lou Lou and Pea called *Cats, Hats, and Bats*. It showed cats of all colors and sizes in elaborate head wear. Calicos wore hats piled high with fruit, black cats sported feathered berets, and Persian cats wore wide-brimmed hats with elaborate curlicues. Around their heads fluttered dark bats. Both Lou Lou and Pea counted this mural among their favorites. Pea liked it because she adored felines and fashion. Lou Lou loved the bats, which were a horticulturist's friend thanks to their appetite for pests and their ability to pollinate plants and flowers.

But today at *Cats, Hats, and Bats*, Lou Lou stared at a new addition to the mural. Between two Himalayan cats in sombreros stood a familiar woman in glasses. The painter had used careful brushstrokes to make her look wet, adding stringy hair and clothes that hung limply and dripped water.

"Hello, Sugar Skulls Sarah," Lou Lou said to the painting. She wasn't surprised by the image. She'd expected to see Sarah in a mural ever since the suspicious sprinkler storm. Lou Lou pulled the Mural Mystery Matrix from her satchel. She leaned against the wall and added another row to the Matrix, printing *Sugar Skulls Sarah's Sprinkler Storm*. Then she added a column for *Cats, Hats, and Bats* and put an *X* at the intersection of the two. When she was done, she stepped back to survey the mural.

"LOOK AROUND FOR THE BRIGHTEST HUE," Lou Lou quoted from the riddle. "It's gotta be your sweater, Sarah." Sugar Skulls Sarah's sweater was a bright shade of bluish purple. Lou Lou pursed her lips and thought.

"It's indigo!" she exclaimed, pointing one finger in the air at her discovery. She didn't need Pea's color swatch book to confirm this. A few months ago she and Pea had tried to make indigo dye from the leaves of one of Lou Lou's plants to color Pea's handmade skirt. It hadn't worked well and they'd ended up with a wet bundle of grayish cotton. But Lou Lou admired the true color of indigo.

Lou Lou carefully wrote *Indigo* below the new *X* on the Matrix and underlined the *I*.

"Just a few more clues to go!" she announced triumphantly to the afternoon sky.

CHAPTER TWENTY-FOUR
Almrei

Lou Lou ran all the way to *If Pigs Could Fly*. Pea was waiting for her when she arrived with her color swatch book tucked under her arm.

"Hi!" said Lou Lou, panting to catch her breath. "I found something—" She stopped in midsentence. "First, how's Uno?"

"Messy." Pea crinkled her nose. "What did you find?"

"Sugar Skulls Sarah!" Lou Lou replied. "She's in *Cats, Hats, and Bats*! In her indigo sweater." Lou Lou showed Pea the Matrix.

"Poor Sarah," said Pea. "But at least we are making progress on the riddle."

"Speaking of . . ." Lou Lou was looking at the mural.

"Ella Divine is the **SOMETHING NEW** in this one," Pea said. "Her lips are a beautiful shade of scarlet but her emerald gown is definitely the **BRIGHTEST HUE**." Pea flipped her swatch book open to a shade of emerald green that matched the mural.

"Great!" Lou Lou wrote *Emerald* in the correct box on the Matrix and underlined the *E*.

At *School Is for the Birds*, Lou Lou and Pea got right to work on riddle solving. After some consideration, they decided that the **BRIGHTEST HUE** was the lemon color of Magdalena's dress, not the purple stain. Lou Lou wrote *Lemon* in the correct box on the Matrix and underlined the *L*.

"We don't need to go see *Lady Carmen Rides Bonito*," Pea said. "Helado's eyes are definitely the **BRIGHT-EST HUE** in that mural, and we know they are amber."

Lou Lou nodded. "I was thinking the same thing." She added the word *Amber*, also underlining the *A*. "That's it! We've got them all!" Lou Lou held up the Mural Mystery Matrix.

"What do the letters spell?" asked Pea.

"Hmm." Lou Lou read in a diagonal from the top corner of the Matrix to the bottom. "'Almrei.'"

"That's not a real word," Pea pointed out.

"Well, we can't forget about the riddle's P.S.," Lou Lou said. **"YOU SEEK THE ONE THAT'S MISSING.** That has to mean that we're missing a letter! Let's go through the alphabet from *A* to *Z* and try adding each letter to the beginning of *almrei*. Maybe we'll get something that makes sense."

"Sounds like a good strategy to start," said Pea.

"Can you come back to the SS *Lucky Alley* so we can work on it?"

"I am supposed to meet my mother at La Frutería in ten minutes," Pea replied. "She promised to make me a blueberry pie for dessert tonight because I got an A on my History paper about Impressionist painters."

"That's great, Pea!" said Lou Lou. "I really am happy you did well on your Expressionist paper." She paused. "I just wish we could spend more time on the riddle."

"It's *Impressionist*, and thank you," Pea said. "How about we work on the riddle separately tonight to try to find the missing letter? You take *A* through *M*, and I will take *N* through *Z*, and we will call each other if we figure it out."

"Yes!" Lou Lou was happy to keep up the Mural Mystery momentum. As they walked to La Frutería, Pea used Lou Lou's pen to copy *almrei* onto a blank page at the end of her color swatch book. At the fruit store, they said their *see you tomorrow*s and Lou Lou ran all the way back to the SS *Lucky Alley*. She was certain they'd decipher the Mural Mystery riddle and put a stop to the El Corazón crimes once and for all!

CHAPTER TWENTY-FIVE
The One That's Missing

The afternoon turned to evening, and Lou Lou's confidence that she would find the riddle's solution began to wane. She tried adding all the letters from *A* through *M* to the beginning of ALMREI but nothing made sense. BALMREI certainly didn't mean anything. Nor did FALMREI, or any other combination. Lou Lou stared at the Mural Mystery Matrix.

As she ate her dad's castaway chili, she pondered whether the extra letter might go at the end of the word, not the beginning.

"Ahoy, Lou Lou!" Her dad sat down at the table. Lou

Lou's mom was still sick in bed. "Something wrong with the chow?" Lou Lou realized she'd paused in midbite. Beans were sliding off her spoon and making little splashes in her bowl.

"No, sorry, Dad. It's great." Lou Lou quickly folded up the Matrix.

"What are you working on?" her dad asked.

"Just my chart project," Lou Lou said, hoping to avoid more questions. It seemed to work. Her dad nibbled silently on a piece of corn bread.

"Did you ever thank the new neighbor boy for the book?" he asked suddenly. *Thank him! Ha!* Lou Lou thought. She could hardly imagine thanking Jeremy for anything. Let alone a book intended to mock Pinky's planticide.

"No."

"Try to remember next time you see him," said her dad.

"Yes, Dad," Lou Lou grumbled. Her head ached and she wanted to continue working on the riddle. "I'm finished eating and I'm feeling tired. Is it okay if I go to my room?"

"Don't you want a scuttlebutt sundae? I bought your favorite ice cream—mint chocolate chip."

Lou Lou thought for a moment. "Actually, that sounds great." She wasn't making any progress on the Mural Mystery, and scuttlebutt sundaes were delicious. When she'd scraped the last bit of hot fudge from the bottom of her dish, Lou Lou kissed her dad on the cheek and went up to the crow's nest. She truly was tired and decided it was best to get some sleep and then look at the riddle with fresh eyes. Still, it was frustrating to be so close to the solution but missing one piece.

"I'll figure you out in the morning," she said before she turned out the light.

Despite her exhaustion, Lou Lou had trouble falling asleep. She tossed and turned and when she finally drifted off, she dreamed that Helado was in her garden with Pinky. Suddenly, a flood came from nowhere and they were carried away in a huge wave. Lou Lou screamed and ran after them but it was no use. Helado and her beloved camellia were washed out to sea, leaving Lou Lou all alone. But she could still hear Helado crying, in a very unbunnylike voice, "ALMREI! ALMREI! ALMREI!"

In the morning, Lou Lou felt unsettled. It was the day of the procession, when she should have been focused on remembering Pinky. But they still hadn't solved the Mural Mystery and avenged Pinky's planticide. Lou Lou was slowly getting dressed for school when the phone rang.

"Lou Lou, it's Peacock!" her mom called. Lou Lou scampered to the rope ladder. Her mom placed the phone in the bucket and Lou Lou hauled it up.

"Five minutes maximum," Jane said. "Otherwise, you'll miss your bus." Lou Lou put the phone to her ear.

"Pea! Hi! Did you figure something out?" Lou Lou was too excited to bother with *Good morning* or *How was your blueberry pie?*

"Maybe," Pea said. "But it was Kyle who did the figuring."

"Kyle?" Lou Lou asked. "What does Kyle have to do with anything?"

"I went out early with my father to get pasteles and tea for breakfast," Pea began. Lou Lou wasn't surprised. Pastries were one of the only things that could get Pea right out of bed. "Kyle was at the café and he came over to bother me when I was working on the riddle. He didn't know about the missing-letter theory, of course, and he assumed ALMREI was an anagram. Lou Lou, I think Comet Cop Kyle was correct!"

"If it's an anagram, what does it spell?" Lou Lou asked.

"Elmira," Pea whispered. "It spells *Elmira*."

"Elmira?" Lou Lou was confused. "But what does the Candle Lady—"

Before Lou Lou could finish her sentence, her ears were on fire. The candle shop robbery! It wasn't on the Mural Mystery Matrix because it had never been in a mural. The candle shop robbery was **THE ONE THAT'S MISSING**. They were supposed to seek the missing *crime*, not a missing letter. But why? What was special about poor Elmira losing her money and her chance to go on the Candle Lady Caribbean Cruise? Lou Lou suddenly had another thought that seemed too outrageous to be true.

"Pea, is Elmira the Mural Mystery culprit?" she asked. Even as Lou Lou said this, she was thinking it couldn't be possible. Elmira was their friend.

"At first I didn't think so," replied Pea. "But then I considered it some more—"

"She can't be. She's always trying to help everyone," Lou Lou interrupted. "She sold you the Belleza candle

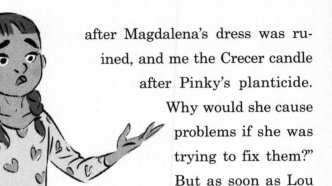

after Magdalena's dress was ruined, and me the Crecer candle after Pinky's planticide. Why would she cause problems if she was trying to fix them?"

But as soon as Lou Lou asked the question, she knew the answer.

"Because more problems means . . ." Pea began.

"More candle sales!" Lou Lou finished.

Lou Lou felt like sparks were shooting out from the sides of her head. It was true that Elmira always had a candle recommendation and had made successful sales after misfortune befell the victims of the neighborhood criminal. Lou Lou pictured Danielle with the Encontrar candle, Elmira had mentioned that Ella Divine would want a Perdón candle, and the Candle Lady had gone to Sarah's Studio to sell her a Reparar candle. Lou Lou wasn't certain if Rosa had bought a candle to ensure Helado's safe return, but she wouldn't be surprised if she had. More problems clearly meant more business for Elmira. It must be true—it had been Elmira all along!

"Time to get off the phone," Lou Lou's mom yelled just as Lou Lou heard Silvia Pearl call, "¡Es hora de colgar el teléfono!"

"Sounds like we both have to go," said Lou Lou. "I wish we didn't have school today!"

"Me too," Pea replied. "But we will talk more this afternoon!"

When Lou Lou hung up the phone, her head was spinning. No wonder the Candle Lady always knew people's problems. It wasn't just because of her "intuition"—she was the criminal! And working with Jeremy, no doubt.

Lou Lou was still sure there was something off about him. She remembered the candle he'd had at Halloween that clearly came from Elmira's shop. And the phone call she'd overheard in the garden. Jeremy must have been talking to Elmira! He was definitely the Candle Lady's henchman—after all, the trouble had started when he arrived in town.

Before she headed off to catch her bus, Lou Lou went to her little window. She could see the bare patch of earth beneath the avocado tree illuminated by the morning sun.

"I know I've found your killers, Pinky," she said under her breath. "And you can bet your heavenly autumn queen blooms that I'm going to prove it!"

CHAPTER TWENTY-SIX
Procession Preparation

All day, Lou Lou had the distinct feeling that the unfortunate and mysterious events of the past few weeks were coming to a climax. It was Día de los Muertos, they had solved the riddle, and they were going to expose the culprit behind the Mural Mystery! She wasn't sure how they were going to pull off the last part, but Lou Lou was confident she and Pea would figure it out.

Pea lived on the other side of El Corazón in a blue house with a big picture window and a cherry tree in the front yard. The Pearl residence was closer than the

SS *Lucky Alley* to the start of the procession, so Lou Lou and Pea decided to get ready there. After school, Lou Lou stopped at home to pick up Pinky's altar, the procession outfits, and flowers from her garden. On the drive to Pea's, Lou Lou tied the flowers into a colorful crown.

She couldn't wait to talk to Pea about the Mural Mystery, but when Lou Lou arrived, she remembered her Pearl-house niceties. Lou Lou removed her shoes, washed her hands, and said a polite hello to Silvia and

Henry Pearl before she rushed to Pea's room. Dos yowled at her from the end of the neatly made bed, but Lou Lou ignored him. As Lou Lou took their procession outfits from her bag, she explained her theory that Jeremy was Elmira's partner in crime.

"They *have* to be working together, Pea. I think Elmira is in charge, but Jeremy is helping her with the evil deeds!"

"That's possible," Pea said.

"Elmira must have staged the candle shop robbery so we wouldn't suspect her," Lou Lou added. She had thought this through during Math. "Remember how none of the glass candleholders were broken? That's because the shelves weren't pushed over by a thief. Elmira did it herself and was careful not to damage anything!"

"No wonder she wanted to clean up the crime scene *before* the police came," Pea said. "I just thought she was being tidy, but now I am sure she never actually reported the robbery since it wasn't real!" After a moment, Pea added, "It's sad that Elmira is a criminal. I always thought she was kind."

"I know. Me too," Lou Lou replied. "I still don't think she has *only* mean bones in her body." It was difficult to admit this about Pinky's killer, but during Social

Studies, Lou Lou had thought about all the nice things Elmira had done for them. Like how she'd given Lou Lou a Feliz Cumpleaños candle for her seventh birthday. Or brought Pea a Sanar candle to speed up the healing when she'd broken her arm. "But I guess we never saw all sides of the Candle Lady."

"So what should we do next?" Pea asked as she changed into her colorful butterfly skirt and blue sweater.

"We definitely need to find evidence of her crimes so we can expose her!"

"Maybe we can even get Helado back for Rosa," said Pea.

"Elmira always goes out during the procession to sell candles from her cart." Lou Lou pulled on her flowered dress. "That would be a good time to sneak into the candle shop. Can you zip me up?"

"We will have to be careful," said Pea. "She can't know that we're on to her before we can prove she is responsible. Otherwise she'll try to cover everything up so no one believes us. Remember that's what happened in the mystery we read during the summer? The jewel thief hid all the rubies and diamonds before the police came!"

Lou Lou nodded. "Let's bring Pinky's altar and start walking in the procession, at least until Twenty-Third Street." As eager as she was to catch Elmira, she wanted some of the evening to be dedicated to Pinky's memory. "Then we can make up an excuse to tell Magdalena and go to the candle shop."

By now Lou Lou and Pea were dressed, so it was time to transform into skeletons. First, a wash of white makeup turned their faces to bones. Pea carefully colored her lips black and drew on dark eye sockets with the black liner, which made the blue of her eyes pop.

"Now do me," Lou Lou said when Pea's makeup was complete. "You're so good and I always mess it up." Pea used the liner to make Lou Lou's face a mirror image of her own. They added the finishing touches to their Día de los Muertos outfits—Lou Lou's hat, Pea's parasol, and Pinky's altar. Lou Lou handed Pea the flower crown she'd made.

"So you have something pretty for your hair," Lou Lou said. Pea placed the crown on her head and smiled.

"¡Gracias, Lou Lou! It's beautiful. You made it exactly the way I taught you!"

Lou Lou grabbed her satchel and her little green

camera, which had been a tenth-birthday present. They went into the living room where Pea's parents were reading.

"Oh my! Look at you two!" Henry exclaimed. He took a quick photograph with Lou Lou's camera.

"Lou Lou, that is a beautiful way to honor Pinky's memory." Pea's mother pointed at the altar. "¿Tienen hambre? I made fresh tamales for Día de los Muertos." Lou Lou fidgeted. She loved Silvia's tamales, but she was eager to get going.

"Gracias, Mamá, pero no tenemos tiempo," Pea replied.

"I thought you might be in a hurry so I made you cucumber sandwiches just in case." Silvia held out a paper bag, which Lou Lou put into her satchel.

"Thank you!" she said.

"De nada," replied Silvia. "We will be watching the procession from the Padillas' balcony with the Bombays, so call if you need anything."

"Claro. Hasta luego," Pea said to her parents, kissing each of them on the cheek.

"Yes, hasta luego!" Lou Lou chimed in.

When they opened the front door, Magdalena was already waiting on the porch. She wore a long dress and carried marigolds and a white candle. Magdalena flashed her gold-medal smile.

"¿Listas, chicas?" she asked.

Lou Lou took a deep breath. Her ears were already tingling.

"Ready," she and Pea answered together.

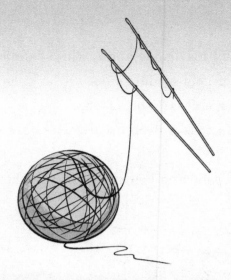

CHAPTER TWENTY-SEVEN
Día de los Muertos
(Part One)

That night, a different world waited for Lou Lou and Pea in El Corazón. Crowds of people, some with painted skeleton faces, talked in groups or quietly gathered around altars on the sidewalks. The air was filled with the smoky perfume of incense, and it looked as if a rainbow had exploded. Strings of red papel picado—tissue paper flags with cut-out designs—fluttered in the light wind. Orange and yellow marigolds filled vases, tin cups, and glass jars. Little blue and green lights framed an altar dedicated to someone's beloved auntie Maribel. A man strummed a purple guitar, softly singing a love song to a photograph of a beautiful woman.

Lou Lou and Pea took in the sights, sounds, and smells, stopping to marvel at altars or say their hellos to friends and neighbors. Lou Lou held Pinky's altar proudly. She tried to clear her mind of the Mural Mystery for a few moments to remember Pinky in full bloom on a sunny day, thriving under the protection of the avocado tree. Lou Lou pictured her beloved camellia decorated with thousands of Flowering Bushes and Shrubs blue ribbons in an afterlife plant paradise.

Magdalena walked beside Pea but stopped when she saw a group of her friends.

"¿Espera aquí, bien?" she asked.

"Of course," Pea replied, agreeing to wait for her.

While Magdalena was with her friends, Lou Lou and Pea wandered over to an altar adorned with flowered vines and hearts made from different shades of yarn. A man was knitting nearby in a ring of candles.

"Hi, Thomas," Lou Lou said. Thomas from Sparkle 'N Clean looked up from his knitting needles, puzzled. "It's Lou Lou and Peacock," she added. The skeleton makeup made it difficult to recognize them.

"Darlings! Good evening! Nice to see you," Thomas replied.

"Who are you remembering tonight?" Pea pointed at the altar. In the midst of the elaborate yarn designs was a picture of a woman in a rocking chair.

"My mother," replied Thomas. "She taught me how to knit. It was her favorite pastime."

Lou Lou was about to compliment Thomas's altar when she saw blue spikes in the distant crowd.

"Jeremy!" she hissed, and tugged on Pea's sweater. Of course he's here, thought Lou Lou. Probably looking for another victim. "Let's follow him. Maybe he'll meet up with Elmira and then we'll know it's safe to go to the candle shop."

Pea asked, "But what about Magda—"

"Don't worry, we'll find her later!" Sensing Pea's hesitation, Lou Lou said, "Thomas, if you see Magdalena, can you please tell her we're fine, we just went to help a friend?" This wasn't exactly a lie—they *were* helping friends by solving the Mural Mystery.

"Of course," Thomas replied. Lou Lou gave Pea a *will that do?* look. Pea nodded.

"Thanks, Thomas! Let's go!" Lou Lou called over her shoulder. Pea hurried after her.

They waded through a sea of people all making their way toward the starting point of the procession. Lou

Lou caught glimpses of Jeremy but she kept losing him in the crowd. By the time the procession began, he'd disappeared altogether.

Sugar Skulls Sarah led the way. She'd managed to remake many of her skulls after the sprinkler storm, but they weren't as elaborate as in years past. Lou Lou noticed one of Elmira's candles in the back of Sarah's wagon. The glass holder showed a picture of a painter's palette and read *Creativo*. It was the same candle that Lou Lou had bought before the third-grade writing contest. Sarah had likely hoped it would help her speedily craft the replacement sugar skulls.

"Jeremy! Over there!" Lou Lou spotted her neighbor half a block away. "Let's go to the edge of the procession so we can get a better view of what he's doing." Without waiting for Pea to answer, Lou Lou tucked Pinky's altar under her arm and grabbed Pea's hand. They wove through the mass of brightly colored skeletons. When they finally made it to the sidewalk, they nearly collided with Danielle Desserts and her snooty-girl posse.

"Hey, watch it!" said Danielle. She was wearing a bubblegum-colored dress and her face was painted only with her usual lip gloss. Apparently, she didn't do skeletons.

"Sorry," Pea said. Lou Lou noticed Danielle was holding a candle that said *Amor*.

"Did you *just* buy that candle, Danielle?" Lou Lou asked.

"I might have," replied Danielle. "Why do you care?"

"Her crush is here tonight so she wanted a loooove candle," one of her friends blabbed. Danielle shot her a dirty look.

"You must have seen Elmira to get the candle. Where is she?" Lou Lou asked.

"She's right across the street." Danielle surprised Lou Lou with a straight answer for once. Lou Lou caught a glimpse of the Candle Lady pushing a cart loaded with candles. This meant that Elmira's shop was empty.

"Thanks, Danielle. I appreciate—"

"Whatever. You helped me look for my necklace so we're even, got it? Now get out of here!" Danielle turned her back to Lou Lou, who was more than happy to move on.

"We have to get to the candle shop quickly!" Pea said. "Before Elmira returns to reload her cart."

They ducked down a side street to escape the crowd. But there were people everywhere blocking their way.

As she scanned for the quickest route, Lou Lou saw blue spikes at the other end of the street.

"There he is!" she exclaimed.

"Just forget about him," Pea said. "Now that we know Elmira's whereabouts, we don't need to follow Jeremy."

Lou Lou knew she was right. The most important thing was getting to the candle shop. Lou Lou turned a few more corners, but when she glanced behind her, there were the blue spikes again.

"Pea! I think *he's* following *us!*" Lou Lou said.

Pea looked over her shoulder. Sure enough, Jeremy was now behind them.

"This way!" Pea led her best friend down an alley to a larger street. When Lou Lou glanced back, she saw that Jeremy had made the same turn.

"He's on to us!" Lou Lou said. "He's going to stop us from finding evidence!" They zigzagged through more skeletons, trying to lose Jeremy. But it seemed impossible—he stayed close on their tail! Lou Lou was looking around for a place to hide when Pea pulled her into the doorway of a taqueria.

"Try the enchiladas verdes. They're the best in town," a woman advised before she left the taqueria.

"Gracias," Pea said politely as blue spikes streaked past and disappeared into the crowd.

"Quick thinking, Pea! He's gone!" Lou Lou said.

Now that they were Jeremy-free, it was high time to get to the candle shop and crack the Mural Mystery once and for all.

CHAPTER TWENTY-EIGHT
Día de los Muertos
(Part Two)

Arriving at the candle shop, Lou Lou felt her nerves grow jumpy. What if they couldn't find any evidence and, instead, got in trouble for entering without Elmira's permission? Not to mention, they didn't have a plan for what to do once they were inside the shop or even how to get inside in the first place. Lou Lou pushed hopefully on the door. Locked.

"Shoot! Any ideas?" she asked Pea. For the first time, Lou Lou thought that maybe an adult or the police might have come in handy. "We can't break the glass. We'd be grounded forever, even if Elmira is the culprit!"

"Not to mention how dangerous that would be. We can try the back door," Pea suggested. "Remember what Elmira said after the fake robbery?"

"'Sometimes I forget to lock the back when I close the shop,'" Lou Lou quoted the Candle Lady. "Brilliant!"

They darted through the narrow alley between Manny's Bodega and the candle shop to the back door. Lou Lou crossed her fingers and turned the knob.

Unlocked!

She raised her eyebrows at Pea, and Pea nodded. Together they entered the shop's back room. Lou Lou stashed her hat and Pinky's altar in a corner along with Pea's parasol.

"I can check the candle shelves for evidence while you search her desk," Pea suggested. Although the candles were mostly arranged in neat rows, Pea began straightening out stray candles.

"How about *I* check the candle shelves while *you* search her desk?" Lou Lou suggested. "If you tidy things, she'll know someone has been here."

"Good point." Pea reluctantly messed up her work so that the candles were returned to their original positions.

Lou Lou wove her way through the shelves but nothing seemed out of the ordinary. She peeked behind the candle rows but there was no sign of anything at all except for dust and a runaway peppermint candy.

When Lou Lou was halfway through her search, Pea called out, "Come look at this!" Lou Lou joined Pea at Elmira's small desk. It was covered in a mess of papers that Pea was clearly trying hard not to organize. The paper in Pea's hand said:

Official Ticket, Candle Lady Caribbean Cruise! Issued to Elmira the Candle Lady for a luxury suite and special VIP reception with Lydia Luz!

Next to Elmira's desk was an open suitcase overflowing with summer clothes, a swimsuit, and sunglasses.

"So she's going on her Candle Lady Caribbean Cruise after all!" Lou Lou said.

"Yes," replied Pea. "That is probably why she committed the crimes. To sell more candles to pay for her trip!"

"But the ticket alone is not proof that Elmira is the culprit. There has to be something else, Pea!" Lou Lou said.

"Okay, but we're running out of time to investigate. Elmira will be back from the procession soon!" Pea replied.

Lou Lou and Pea searched frantically for more evidence. That was when Lou Lou noticed something odd. Between two Valentía, or courage, candles on a far shelf, she could just make out a word written on the wall. She squinted at it and read, *Sótano*. Lou Lou recognized the Spanish but the meaning escaped her. She opened her mouth to ask Pea, when suddenly it came to her—Pea's laughter in the front hallway of the SS *Lucky Alley* when Lou Lou confused the Spanish word for sailor with *sótano*, the word for cellar. That was it— cellar! And a cellar, thought Lou Lou, is a perfect place for the Candle Lady to hide her secrets.

"Pea, I think I found the cellar! I'm just not sure how to get inside." Lou Lou searched for a way in but she couldn't find a knob to turn or a panel to push. Pea appeared by her side.

"How odd," Pea said. "One of these Valentía candles looks different from the others. Almost like a fake." Pea grasped the candle to pull it from the shelf but it didn't budge. Instead the whole shelf swung toward her. It was a door to the cellar with a candle handle!

"Amazing!" said Lou Lou, who only wasted a moment wishing Elmira wasn't their enemy so she could show Lou Lou how to make a secret door for the SS *Lucky Alley*. "Let's go!"

Lou Lou and Pea slipped through the hidden door, closing it behind them. They quietly made their way down a dimly lit staircase to another door at the bottom. Lou Lou looked at Pea, took a deep breath, and turned the knob, hoping their lock luck would hold out. But this door was bolted shut. Lou Lou's ears were hot little coals against her head and she jiggled the knob, willing the lock to give. Then, from the other side of the door, came a *thump, thump, thump* that made Lou Lou freeze in mid-jiggle. Pea grabbed Lou Lou's hand.

"Someone or something is in there!" she whispered. "What should we do?" They heard the noise again.

"Hello?" Lou Lou called through the door. "Who's there?" No answer came, just more thumping.

Pea squeezed Lou Lou's hand harder. "Maybe we should go back," she said.

Lou Lou knew Pea was probably right. Even though she wanted to find out what was behind the door, it was too risky. It might be an angry attack dog guarding Elmira's secret cellar. Or worse, the thumping was Elmira herself, working on another sinister plan after beating them to the candle shop. Lou Lou turned to go back up the stairs. But then she thought about poor Pinky and her promise to avenge her camellia's death.

"We can do this," she said under her breath and

jiggled the knob one final time. Something gave, and the door opened a crack.

THUMP, THUMP, THUMP!

The noise was louder now. With Pea still gripping one hand, Lou Lou used the other to slowly push open the door. She raised her arm in defense against a vicious canine and prepared to let loose a stream of excuses to the Candle Lady about why they were on her cellar stairs. But instead of a dog's snarl or Elmira's face, Lou Lou saw a little white bunny with amber eyes stomping one back foot.

"Helado!" Lou Lou gasped. As she entered the cellar, the bunny scurried away. Pea came in behind her and closed the cellar door. She crouched down and clicked her tongue at Helado. Lou Lou had seen her do the same thing to soothe Uno and Dos. The bunny ceased its thumping and bounded over to Pea.

"He's friendly!" Pea said. "He was probably just scared because he thought we were Elmira." She patted the bunny's head.

Lou Lou looked around the cellar. The space was almost entirely filled with stacked candle boxes marked VELAS. In one corner were food and water dishes for poor bunnynapped Helado. In the other was a table covered in a hodgepodge of items. There were powders and potions, junk and jewelry, including a necklace adorned with four rose-gold stars.

"Danielle's best-friends shining-star necklace!" Lou Lou said. A row of bottles sat on a shelf over the table. Lou Lou picked up one that held a purple liquid and smelled it.

"One part grape juice . . ." Lou Lou said.

". . . two parts DYE!" Pea finished. "That must be what made the stain on Magdalena's dress!"

"This one smells like bleach," Lou Lou said, sniffing another bottle and thinking of Pinky.

"Look! Elmira used this to embarrass Ella Divine during her performance." Pea pointed to a record labeled *"Feathered Fedora," Broken Version*. Lou Lou pulled her camera from her satchel and took a few photos of the stolen and sinister items.

"Evidence!" she said. Suddenly, Lou Lou heard a door slam upstairs, followed by voices. From Pea's wide eyes and Helado's resumed thumping, Lou Lou could tell that they had heard it, too.

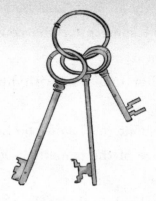

CHAPTER TWENTY-NINE
Día de los Muertos (Fin)

"We have to get out of here," Lou Lou whispered urgently. She stuffed her camera and Danielle's necklace into her satchel.

"We can't go back up the stairs. We will run into whoever is up there," Pea said. And whoever was up there was getting closer to the sótano door. Lou Lou recognized the male voice instantly.

"Jeremy!" she said. The softer female voice was difficult to hear, but Lou Lou assumed it was Elmira.

"I tried to follow Lou Lou but I lost her somewhere during the procession. I'm sorry," Jeremy said.

"He's talking about me!" Lou Lou whispered. The female voice said something she couldn't make out. Jeremy spoke again.

"Yeah, the other one was with her, too. Peacock, right?"

"He's talking about you!" said Lou Lou.

"Oh, I took care of the camellia. Don't worry about that," Jeremy said.

"He's talking about Pinky!" The color of Lou Lou's ears matched the bright red of her sneakers. She still couldn't hear the woman's replies, but she was more certain than ever that Jeremy was the Candle Lady's accomplice.

Then Jeremy said, "I thought they'd figured it out, too. I tried to help them."

Now Lou Lou was confused. Why would Jeremy, one of the criminals, want to help them?

"Pea, I don't—"

"Shh," Pea cautioned. The voices were even closer now.

"We'll have to find a different way," the woman's voice said. "If only I could get him back. Quick, look around to see if he's here." Now Lou Lou could tell it wasn't Elmira speaking. Still, the voice was familiar . . .

"Rosa!" Lou Lou exclaimed.

"What?" asked Pea.

"It's Rosa up there with Jeremy!"

"Rosa? I thought she was on our side." Before Lou Lou could reply, the talking stopped and she heard the back door open.

"Hola. What are you doing here?" Elmira had arrived. "Poking around without my permission, I presume! Looking for a bunny, perhaps?"

"Please, please return my pet," Rosa pleaded. "We haven't told anyone about your crimes. You know that— you've been watching us all the time."

"Yeah, c'mon. Just give him back to Rosa. And stop all this mischief. You've done enough damage." This was Jeremy speaking. It was an odd choice of words for Elmira's accomplice. Then Lou Lou had a startling thought. What if Jeremy was one of the good guys?

"Pea, I might have been wro—"

"Yes, I know. Sounds like he has been on our side all along." Pea saved Lou Lou from admitting her mistake.

"You know I can't give that bunny back," Lou Lou heard Elmira say. "And you're loco if you think I can stop now. It's true that I only planned to make enough money to pay for my Candle Lady Caribbean Cruise so

I could finally rest my tired bones on vacation. But now that I have made reservations for the Candle Lady Chalet Getaway and the Candle Lady Carnival in the spring, I must continue my work."

"Tía, how can you be so cruel?" It sounded like Rosa was crying now.

"Our abuelo would be ashamed if he knew how you were treating Rosa and the shop's loyal customers," Jeremy said. "What happened to the kind and helpful tía that I knew as a little kid? How did you become so coldhearted?" Lou Lou and Pea exchanged glances. ¿Tía? ¿Abuelo? Were Elmira, Rosa, and Jeremy related?

"It's not like I enjoy hurting people, mis queridos," Elmira said. "I love to help with everyone's problems, but it's important that my customers have *enough* problems so that I can solve them with a sale. That's why you can't tell anyone about my little pranks. You should have taken the share of the profits I kindly offered you to keep quiet. You wouldn't believe how many customers have fallen for my scheme. It has been a smashing success!"

"We don't want your money. We want to do the right thing, Tía," Rosa said.

"Hacerlo correcto," Elmira mocked Rosa. "You made

a bad decision, niña. If you'd accepted my money, I wouldn't have taken your pet to ensure your silence. And I know about those tricks you played painting the murals. Too bad no one really pays attention to the details except for those silly little girls."

Lou Lou had had enough. It was one thing for Elmira to dismiss all the troubles she'd caused in El Corazón as "little pranks." It was quite another for her to call Lou Lou and Pea *silly* or *little*. Without bothering with her *chrysanthemum*s, Lou Lou raced up the stairs. Pea was right behind her and Helado bounded at Pea's heels. Lou Lou threw open the sótano door and was met by three very surprised faces.

"Now you listen here, Elmira the Candle Lady. We know everything! You ruined Magdalena's dress and stole Danielle's necklace. You embarrassed Ella Divine and melted all the sugar skulls. You bunnynapped Helado. And worst of all, you killed Pinky! You're the silly one if you think you are getting away with this, because we have proof that you're the Mural Mystery culprit!"

As if he knew that *proof* was his cue, Helado jumped from behind Pea straight into Rosa's arms. The surprise on Rosa's face changed instantly to a beaming smile.

"¡Mi mascota!" Rosa kissed the bunny's ears. "I can't believe it's really you, safe and sound."

"We have photos and evidence of your other crimes, too, Elmira," Pea said. Lou Lou fished Danielle's necklace and her camera from her satchel.

"You're busted, Tía Elmira!" Jeremy said.

The color drained from Elmira's face and she looked crumpled, like someone had let all the air out of her.

"Give me the keys to the shop, Tía," said Rosa. It was the first time Lou Lou had heard her raise her soft voice. "Leave now and maybe you will suffer no further punishment for your bad deeds."

Jeremy closed Elmira's suitcase and handed it to her. "Good thing you're already packed."

Elmira faced the small group. Lou Lou swore she saw the Candle Lady's eyes watering. She dropped the keys to the shop on the floor and edged toward the exit.

"I am truly sorry about your camellia, Lou Lou Bombay," Elmira said, actually sounding sincere. With that, she turned and bolted, banging the door behind her.

Lou Lou stared at where the Candle Lady had been. She felt a little bad for Elmira but *only* a little. She may have been a good person once, but now she'd inflicted too many tragedies on El Corazón.

Pea picked up the keys to the shop and handed them to Rosa.

"So Elmira is your aunt?" Pea asked Rosa and Jeremy.

"You got it!" Jeremy said.

"This candle shop has been in our family for years,"

Rosa explained. "Our grandfather left it to me when he died and Tía Elmira was supposed to manage it until I was old enough to take it over. At first, she was a great candle lady, but when business was slow, she started spying on people to find out about their problems and sell them candles."

"That makes sense. I always wondered how she knew about Uno and Dos's feline feud," Pea said to Lou Lou.

"Then it got worse when she started hurting people," Rosa added.

"Hurting people *and* plants." Lou Lou made sure Pinky was not forgotten.

"Right, people and plants and animals, too," Rosa said.

"And you didn't tell anyone about her crimes because she was threatening your bunny?" Pea asked.

"Exactamente. She told me I would never see my pet again if I revealed her secrets. She was always watching me and Jeremy. We didn't even dare to speak her name out loud. And we also didn't want to bring shame on our family's candle shop by telling the world that our tía was a bad person. Our beloved abuelo worked hard to build this business. It wouldn't have been fair to him to tarnish the shop's reputation."

"Plus, it would have been difficult to convince our

family to believe us without proof," Jeremy added. "Elders like Tía Elmira are respected in our family. We couldn't just go around accusing her of things. We had no idea she was keeping all the evidence in a secret cellar until you two popped out of it!"

"But you thought if someone could figure out for themselves that Elmira was the culprit, they could help you without her suspecting and without making a big fuss that would hurt the shop." It was all making sense now. "That's why you changed the murals," Lou Lou said.

"Yes!" replied Rosa. "And my primo, Jeremy, thought up the riddle."

"I love riddles!" Jeremy said, and made a funny face. Lou Lou rolled her eyes at his goofiness, but she couldn't help smiling. It seemed she and Jeremy had something in common after all.

"That's why he had Rosa's phone number. Because they are cousins," Pea whispered to Lou Lou. And the phone conversation that she'd overheard must have been with Rosa, not Elmira, thought Lou Lou.

"So when I saw you at the crafts store you were buying paint for Rosa?" Lou Lou asked.

"Spying on me, eh?" said Jeremy. "Not very neighborly." He winked good-naturedly. "That's right."

"And our plan with the murals seemed to be working." Rosa picked up her story where she'd left off. "We were relieved that you two noticed them and wanted to solve the mystery on your own! But at the end, I suspected Tía Elmira knew what was going on. That's why I asked Jeremy to keep an eye on you during the procession, to make sure you were okay."

"I think it's my fault that she knew," Lou Lou said. "I told Elmira about the murals because I wanted her advice."

"She fooled everyone into trusting her," said Rosa. "What's important is that you stopped her from committing more crimes—and you saved my dear mascota. Thank you so much, Lou Lou Bombay and Peacock Pearl. I will be forever grateful to you."

"Yeah, thanks!" Jeremy said.

"De nada," said Pea.

"It was no big deal," Lou Lou added, even though she knew it really was a very big deal.

They all stood silent for a moment. Lou Lou's stomach was growling since she'd forgotten to eat her sandwich. Her eyes stung from the black skeleton makeup that had run during their earlier game of dodge-Jeremy, and she was exhausted from all the excitement.

"Head home for cake and cocoa?" Lou Lou asked Pea just as Pea's phone rang.

"¿Magdalena?" Pea answered. "¡Lo siento, lo siento! No, I didn't hear my phone ring before. Sí, estamos en the candle shop." Pea hung up. "We'd better go. Magdalena is coming to walk with us. Would you care to join us for a snack?" she asked Jeremy and Rosa politely.

"That's very nice of you, but we are supposed to meet up with our family," Rosa said. "Perhaps another time."

Lou Lou and Pea said goodbye to Rosa and Jeremy. Rosa even put Helado down to hug them both. Lou Lou fetched her hat, Pinky's altar, and Pea's parasol, and they were heading for the candle shop's back door when Pea turned around and called to Rosa.

"What's the bunny's real name?"

Rosa smiled. "I was calling him Ralph. But I like Helado much better. Yes, he will be Helado from now on."

CHAPTER THIRTY
PSPP

During the week after Día de los Muertos, Lou Lou and Pea did their best to discreetly remedy the harms caused by Elmira. Lou Lou slipped Danielle's necklace back into her purse. During lunch she saw Danielle pull it out and squeal with pleasure.

"It worked!" Danielle said. "The Encontrar candle helped me find my necklace!"

Lou Lou and Pea told Ella Divine that she wouldn't have to worry about any more broken records, and the singer assured them she would never lip-synch again. They informed Magdalena that her future gowns were safe from suspicious stains, and told Sugar Skulls Sarah there would be no meltdown before next year's Día de los Muertos. When Elmira's victims asked Lou Lou and Pea how they knew these things, Lou Lou said, "Tengo la intuición."

Now it was 3:37 p.m. on Friday, and Lou Lou Bombay was where she belonged—in her sunlit garden, lovingly tending to her plants and flowers.

She heard a knock at the backyard gate. A small brown-haired girl wearing a crisp school uniform was standing outside.

"Hi, Pea! I mean, welcome to my humble garden, Miss Peacock Pearl!" Lou Lou remembered to greet her best friend with the customary PSPP formality.

"Thank you, Miss Lou Lou Bombay! I am very pleased to be here," Pea said.

"I do hope your journey was not long," said Lou Lou.

"Not at all," Pea replied with a dismissive wave. "Shall we?"

And so began another PSPP. Lou Lou and Pea sat

down to tea and scones. Now that they'd solved the Mural Mystery, Pinky's killer had left town, and the rest of El Corazón was safe from Elmira, Lou Lou felt happy in her horticultural haven behind the SS *Lucky Alley*. All was quiet and calm. At least until a spiky blue head poked over the fence.

"Hiya, Lou Lou and Peacock," Jeremy said. "Just wanted to tell you that I'm not gonna be your neighbor for much longer. The old guy is coming back from Toledo."

"What? You're moving already?" Lou Lou asked. "I mean, okay, whatever." She tried to sound like she didn't care, but Lou Lou was sad about losing Jeremy as a neighbor. Sure, he was strange, but he was also amusing and had turned out to be pretty nice. Not just fake friendly.

"Don't be heartbroken about it. My parents found a house a few blocks away. You're not getting rid of me." Jeremy winked.

"We are happy to have met you and we do hope to see you again soon," Pea said with PSPP politeness. "May I offer you a blueberry scone?"

"Naw, but thanks," replied Jeremy. "I prefer currant. I make really good ones, actually. Better than my cookies! Maybe I'll bake you guys some next week. But I gotta go pack now." Jeremy looked at Lou Lou. "Take good care of Punky."

"I think you mean Pinky. And, as you know, dear Pinky is no longer with us." Lou Lou wondered how he could have forgotten after all that had happened.

"Nope, I mean *Punky*. It's what I named the rowdy rebel variety camellia that I planted for you under the avocado tree." Lou Lou stared openmouthed at Jeremy, then ran to the tree and looked closely. Sure enough, a sprout had just pushed its way up through the soil close to where Pinky had once bloomed.

"Don't worry, I fixed the hole in the fence I made to get into your yard." Jeremy pointed at a section of wooden slats. "I left 'em loose in there before so you wouldn't see the gap. But now they're nice and solid."

"You didn't just climb the fence?" Pea asked.

"Gosh, no. You think I don't care about how I look? I already got bleach on my jeans when I was helping my dad do laundry. I didn't want to scuff my boots climbing a silly fence, too."

Pea nodded approvingly, and Jeremy grinned. "Make sure Punky gets regular water," he called to Lou Lou.

"And remember that the ideal soil pH is within the 6.0 to 6.5 range. You probably know everything about camellias, but it's all in that book I gave you, *Caring for Your Camellia*, in case you forget."

"Pea, come look at this!" Lou Lou said. Pea joined her under the tree. Lou Lou thought back on past encounters with Jeremy. She remembered the hammer she'd seen when they first met, his dirty fingernails at Sarah's Studio, and his late-night visit to her garden. What had seemed suspicious at the time, Lou Lou now realized, must have been related to Jeremy's acts of horticultural heroism. A bit of fence tampering with the hammer to do a good deed, perhaps a visit to Green Thumb for camellia seeds and gardening lessons from Juan, and then some moonlight planting in the backyard of the SS *Lucky Alley*.

"So when he told Rosa in the candle shop that he had taken care of the plant, he didn't mean he killed Pinky," Pea said.

"He meant he gave life to Punky!" finished Lou Lou.

Lou Lou ran back over to the fence to peer into her neighbor's yard, but Jeremy wasn't there.

"Can you believe it?" Lou Lou asked. "All this time

I thought . . . and then he . . ." For once, Lou Lou was at a loss for words.

"Guess you've got a chance at a future Hello Horticulture! Society Flowering Bushes and Shrubs blue ribbon after all!" Pea smiled. Lou Lou nodded in amazement.

"Shall we head in now, my dear?" Pea asked formally.

"Um, yes . . . yes, of course," answered Lou Lou, still in shock from the pleasant camellia surprise. She wondered at her budding new friendship with Jeremy as she looked back at the new growth under the tree.

"Happy PSPP, Punky. Until tomorrow . . ."

The girls went inside the SS *Lucky Alley* and put their dishes in the kitchen sink. Then Pea looked at Lou Lou.

"Candles or cupcakes?" she asked. Here was the usual dilemma—should they head to Cupcake Cabana for their favorite frosted treats, or should they pay Rosa the Candle Lady a visit?

Lou Lou looked at a white candle on the kitchen counter. It was a thank-you present from Rosa. There was a picture of a dove on the glass holder and the word

Paz. The candle seemed to be working—peace was exactly what Lou Lou had felt since she and Pea had solved the Mural Mystery.

"Candles," Lou Lou replied. "Definitely candles today."

The End

PEA'S
Pinky Pan de Muerto

·>> INGREDIENTS <<·

For the bread:

- ¼ cup butter (mantequilla)
- ¼ cup whole milk (leche entera)
- ¼ cup water (agua)
- 1 packet yeast (levadura)
- ¼ cup sugar (azúcar)
- ½ teaspoon salt (sal)
- ½ tablespoon cinnamon (canela)
- 2¾ cups flour (harina) plus a little extra for coating the work surface when kneading the dough
- 1 tablespoon orange zest (cáscara de naranja) (optional)
- 2 tablespoons orange blossom water or orange juice (agua de azahar o jugo de naranja) (Pea used orange blossom water in honor of Pinky, but orange juice will work fine!)
- 2 eggs (huevos)

For the topping:

- 3 tablespoons butter (mantequilla)
- Pinky-colored sugar (azúcar rosada) (Pea used magenta, but pink, purple, and/or red will look lovely, too!)

·>> INSTRUCTIONS <<·

1. Before you begin, make sure you have an adult assistant, like Pea's abuela, to help with all the steps involving the oven and the stove.

2. Preheat oven to 350 degrees.

3. Melt the butter, milk, and water in a small saucepan on the stove. Stir gently. Don't let it boil! When the butter is melted, remove the pan from the heat.

4. Combine the yeast, sugar, salt, cinnamon, and ¼ cup of the flour in a bowl. Add the melted-butter mixture, orange zest, and orange blossom water (or orange juice). Mix well. You can use a whisk if you don't have an electric mixer.

5. Mix in each egg. Slowly add the remaining flour in 3 parts, mixing well after each addition.

6. Lightly coat a clean countertop area or cutting board with flour so your dough won't stick to the surface. Knead the dough for 6 to 7 (seis a siete)

minutes. Kneading is hard work! If your arms get tired, ask a family member or best friend to help. Lou Lou sometimes does this part because Pea doesn't like to get her hands dirty!

7. When your dough looks shiny and smooth, separate it into two balls. One ball should be half the size of the other. Put the smaller ball in a bowl in the fridge. You will use this later to make flower-shaped decorations for your bread. Place the larger ball on a greased baking sheet and cover it with a clean towel or plastic wrap. Don't wrap it too tight—your dough needs room to grow! Leave the wrapped dough in a nice warm place to rise. This takes about an hour and a half—so have PSPP tea, tend to your toad lilies, or clean your room while you wait.

8. You will know your dough is ready when it has grown to about twice its original size. Take the smaller dough ball from the fridge and break off pieces to make flower shapes. You can mold thin flat petals and round centers or roll out your dough and use a flower cookie cutter. Decorate the larger loaf with the flowers, rubbing a tiny bit of water on the loaf and on the backs of your

flower shapes to make the shapes stick to the loaf.

9. Time to bake your Pinky Pan de Muerto! Put the bread in the oven and bake for 30 (treinta) minutes. While you're waiting, you can decorate a sugar skull, make a Día de los Muertos outfit, or finish cleaning your room!

10. When the time is up, take the bread from the oven and knock lightly on the loaf. Careful, it's hot! If your bread sounds hollow (hueco), you know it's done. If you don't hear a hollow noise, bake for a few more minutes.

11. Now it's time to make the topping. Melt 3 tablespoons of butter on the stove or on high in the microwave for 30 seconds. Then brush it on the loaf, taking care to avoid touching the butter because it's hot! If you don't have a brush, use a flexible spatula or butter knife to spread the melted butter on the bread.

12. Sprinkle generously with Pinky-colored sugar.

Your Pinky Pan de Muerto is ready (listo)! Make sure to let it fully cool before you eat it or place it by your altar.

LOU LOU'S
Garden Flower Crown

·» MATERIALS «·

- Flowers (Lou Lou used fresh-picked flowers, but fake crafting flowers work well, too!)
- Scissors
- Wire or structured twine (The thicker, the better!)
- Tape
- Ribbon (Lou Lou chose blue for Pea, of course, but pick any color you like!)

·» INSTRUCTIONS «·

1. Wrap the wire around the crown of your head to measure it (approximately 1 to 2 feet), then cut your wire to that length. If your crown is a gift, like the one Lou Lou made for Pea, you can still use your own head to measure. Just adjust the crown to fit the wearer when you add the ribbon in the final step.

2. Make a loop in each end of your wire. Twist the loop around itself a few times to secure the loose

ends of the wire. Do this for both loops. When you're finished, set your wire aside.

3. Trim your flowers so that each bloom has about 2 inches of stem left.

4. Make small bunches of 3 or 4 flowers, like miniature bouquets. Wrap tape around the stems to secure each bunch. Repeat this step until you have 5 or 6 separate bunches.

5. Now pick up your looped wire. Lay one flower bunch against the wire, starting at one end (blooms pointing toward the loop). Tape the stems along the wire, wrapping the tape around several times until the bouquet feels secure. Repeat this step, overlapping the next bunch of flowers with the stems of the first bunch, facing the same direction. Be sure to keep the bunches close together so there aren't any gaps in your crown.

6. When you reach the other end and tape your last bunch on, it's time for ribbon! Thread the ribbon through both loops at the back of the crown. Place the crown on your head, or on the head of your best friend or other wearer. Pull the ribbon tight to fit the crown, and tie a bow to fasten it.

Enjoy your beautiful corona de flores!

LOU LOU & PEA'S
Words to Know in Spanish

Note: Nouns in Spanish carry genders. Sometimes, one noun has two different genders to reflect the subject in question. If the suffix is an *a*, then it's a female noun. If it's an *o*, it's a male noun.

abuela – grandmother

adiós – goodbye

almuerzo – lunch

amiga / amigo – female friend / male friend

   mi amiga / mi amigo – my friend

año(s) – year(s)

artista – artist or performer

bien / buena(o) – well, good

bienvenidas(os) – welcome

bisabuela – great-grandmother

bonita(o) – beautiful

buenas noches – good evening, good night

buenas tardes – good afternoon

calaveras – sugar skulls

camelia – camellia

cena – dinner

chicas / chicos – girls / boys

claro – of course

¿cómo estás (tú) / cómo está (usted)? – how are you?

de nada – you're welcome

desayuno – breakfast

Día de los Muertos – Day of the Dead

flor(es) – flower(s)

gata(o) – cat

gracias – thank you

¡hasta luego! – see you later!

hola – hello

hoy – today

intuición – intuition

lista(o) – ready

lo siento – I'm sorry

luz – light

mamá – mother

mañana – tomorrow

mascota – pet

mucha(s) / mucho(s) – many, a lot

muy bien – very good

niñas / niños – girls / boys

nosotros – we

papá – father

papel picado – cut tissue paper

pasteles – pastries

perdón – excuse me

pero – but, however

perra(o) – dog

por favor – please

preciosa(o) – precious

prima / primo – cousin

problema – problem

quinceañera – fifteenth-birthday
   party

señora / señor – woman / man

sí / no – yes / no

suerte – luck

taqueria – taco shop

teléfono – telephone

tengo – I have

tía / tío – aunt / uncle

tiempo – time

tú – you, informal (friends and siblings)

usted / ustedes – you, formal (parents and adults, singular) / you, formal (parents and adults, plural)

yo – I

·>> ACKNOWLEDGMENTS <<·

Muchas gracias to my amazing editor, Grace Kendall, and my agent extraordinaire, Jennifer Rofé, for their wisdom and insight, good humor, and enthusiasm for Lou Lou and Pea. Also, to everyone else at FSG who made this book a reality. Thank you to my critique group/ band of cheerleaders, and to my friends and family for their feedback and encouragement. To my dad, Stephen Diamond, who has believed in my writing since my first poem in elementary school. Finally, to my husband, Ernst Schoen-René, for being a considerate critic and my biggest fan, and for keeping me sane while encouraging me to be crazy.